HER GUY NEXT DOOR FAKE FIANCÉ

An Echo Ridge Romance

RACHELLE J. CHRISTENSEN

PEACHWOOD Press

Praise for

Rachelle J. Christensen's
Award-winning Novels

Hawaiian Masquerade is the perfect summer read. Set on the beautiful island of Kauai, you will fall in love with the characters, the story line, the setting, and most of all the romance. I would highly recommend this fast-paced, fabulous clean romance.

--Cami Checketts, author of *The Feisty One: A Billionaire Bride Pact Romance*

Christensen has done a magnificent job of putting together an unlikely match and letting it challenge the characters to grow, change, and become better together than they were apart. This is a wonderful, sweet romance that you'll want to stay up to finish.

-Lucy McConnell, author of the *Billionaire Marriage Brokers* series

"SILVER CASCADE SECRETS is an exciting romantic suspense novella ... Great writing, a sweet romance, and an intriguing mystery all rolled into a single story."

—Heather B. Moore *USA Today* Bestselling Author of *Finding Sheba*

"Just in time for fall, ... romantic suspense which will tingle the spine and thrill the heart."

—DESERET NEWS, Melissa Demoux

"...A great read for a lazy Sunday afternoon. I highly recommend."

—Diane Darcy, USA Today bestselling author

"Don't expect to get a lot of sleep...If the thrills of the chase don't get you, the thrills of the heart will."

—J. Scott Savage, author of the Mysteries of Cove Series

"*Diamond Rings are Deadly Things* pulled me right in from the first page and held me captive until the very end. Great characters, a compelling plot, a surprising twist at the end... Rachelle Christensen knows how to craft a great mystery."

—*Tristi Pinkston, author of the Secret Sisters Mysteries*

Also by Rachelle J. Christensen

Other Works by Rachelle

Diamond Rings Are Deadly Things (Wedding Planner Mysteries #1)

Veils and Vengeance (#2)

Proposals and Poison (#3)

The Soldier's Bride (A Music Box Romance #1)

Carve Me a Melody (A Music Box Romance #2)

Hawaiian Masquerade (Burke Billionaire Romance #1)

The Billionaire's Stray Heart (Burke Billionaire Romance #2)

The Refugee's Billionaire (Burke Billionaire Romance #3)

How to Fetch a Fiancé

River Whispers

Hope for Christmas: An Echo Ridge Romance #1

The Kiss Thief: An Echo Ridge Romance #2

The Princess Bride of Riodan: An Echo Ridge Romance #3

Coming Home to Love: An Echo Ridge Romance #4

Novellas:

Silver Cascade Secrets

Double Take

Claire's Christmas Dance

Nonfiction:

What Every 6th Grader Needs to Know: 10
Secrets to Connect Moms & Daughters

Lost Children: Coping with Miscarriage

Free book

Get your free book!

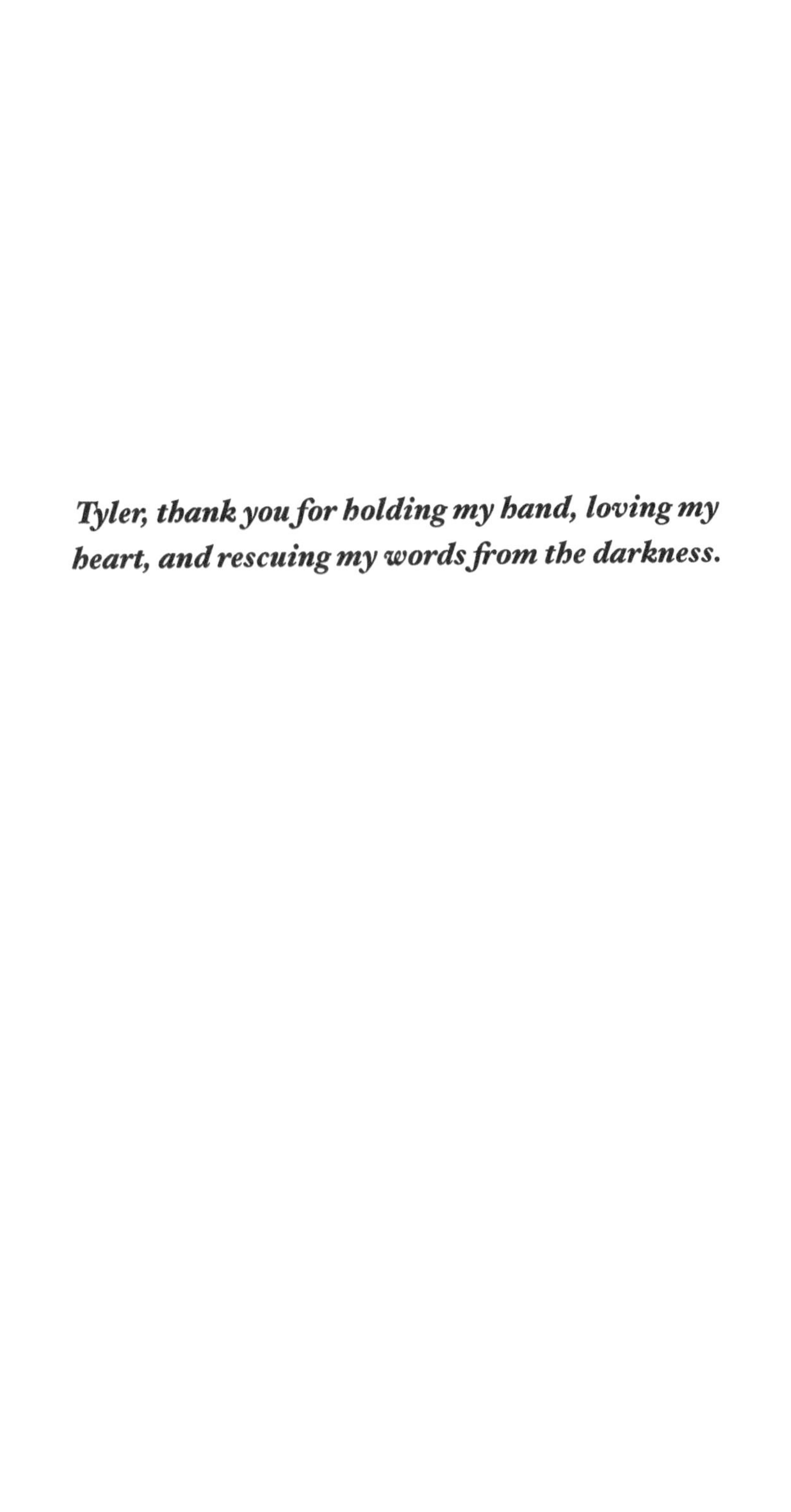

Tyler, thank you for holding my hand, loving my heart, and rescuing my words from the darkness.

Chapter One

The snowfall in Echo Ridge was beautiful—gorgeous snow globe-like flakes floating through the air, dusting the pine trees and making the road through the canyon a slick mess. Liza Sorenson checked the dashboard clock. It said 8:30 a.m., so there was plenty of time to drive carefully out of the canyon and into the heart of Echo Ridge, park in front of Stellar Ads, and set up for her presentation at nine.

"Okay, deep breath," Liza commanded herself. "You've got this." She pumped her brakes as she descended, watching the road for signs of white-tailed deer. The last thing she wanted was to hit a deer on the way to work today. She'd prepared a great presentation on how to easily make over and upgrade websites with copy editing techniques for their new clients. Hopefully, it would amaze her boss enough that he would consider Liza for a promotion.

She tapped the steering wheel of her car with her index finger as she mentally rehearsed the points of her presentation again. The snow was falling steadily and the flakes were sticking to the hood of her blue Ford Fusion, making it look like a speckled Easter egg.

If only they called snow days for work. Liza would stay home, curl up with her laptop, and write. But no, today was important and she would succeed at this job. She gripped the steering wheel tighter as she took the last stretch of road out of the canyon. The bare space on her left ring finger no longer taunted her, but there was still a painful twinge in her heart if she allowed her thoughts to go there.

Instead, she took a moment to appreciate her surroundings. There was a beautiful white two-story house with green shutters that she always admired on her way to work. The guy who lived there was technically her neighbor, but she didn't really know him, although she'd heard rumors that he was a bit of a bad boy. The white fence surrounding the acre of property had an inch of snow balancing along the rails. Everything was dressed in white this morning—the bushes, the trees, the mailbox, the white pickup in the driveway dusted with snow and—

"Noodles!" she screamed as she tried to dodge the pickup backing out of the driveway. She swerved to the right, slamming on her brakes, but the tires had no grip on the ice. The car slid into the side of the pickup with a sickening crunch. Airbags bloomed around Liza's body, and then everything was quiet.

Liza groaned and rubbed the back of her neck, pushing the airbag out of the way. "No! This did not just happen. No!" Her body was stiff and tense, and she reminded herself to breathe. She turned her car off and was fumbling for the door handle when the door opened.

"Are you okay?" a man asked as he crouched down and pushed the airbag out of the way. "Did you hit your head?" He moved aside a lock of her hair, and their eyes met.

Liza stared at him. His eyes were framed with thick lashes, and the scruff on his cheeks made him appear rugged. He wore a gray wool coat with the collar turned up. What had he asked her?

He cocked his head, studying her with those arresting green eyes. "Are you okay?"

Wait. What was happening? She'd been in a wreck, and now she was checking out the guy who had totaled her car. He had asked her if she was okay. She shook her head and closed her eyes, groaning at the stiffness in her body. "No, I'm not all right!"

"Here, let me help you. Where are you hurt?" He reached out his hand—his large, strong hand—and helped her from the car.

She stood blinking as the snowflakes fell on her lashes. "I don't think I'm hurt. Just my neck feels tight.

You pulled out in front of me! I couldn't stop, and then the ice—everything is frozen!"

"I know. I'm sorry. I didn't get all the ice scraped off my windows, and I didn't see you. Are you sure you're not hurt?" He spoke with a musical cadence to his voice, and Liza felt herself leaning towards the low rumble.

This man had wrecked her car. She took a few steps forward to inspect the damage, almost wishing she could cover her eyes so she wouldn't have to see. The headlight on her passenger side was completely smashed and her fender had some serious dents, but it wasn't as bad as she thought—except when she stepped closer and saw that the smashed part of the car had tilted the tire at a weird angle.

"What am I going to do?" Liza turned toward the snowy road. "The cops won't get here for at least twenty minutes, and then it'll take them an hour to cite the accident. I'll miss my presentation!"

The man flinched. "Did you call the cops already?"

"No, I just need to find my phone. Or you can call them." Liza groaned again. "He's gonna fire me." How could this be happening? Just a few minutes ago, she'd been dreaming about getting promoted, and now her quick-to-fire boss would be waiting on her. Rick loved to threaten people with their jobs, and she'd seen enough people get fired to always walk on his right side.

"I'm not going to let you get fired. This is my mess, and I'll clean it up." He pulled his bottom lip between his teeth and then nodded. "I have an idea. You take my pickup to work; I'll get your car into the shop today and get it fixed up. Don't worry about cops and the insurance. I'll take care of everything."

"But—" Liza protested.

"But nothing. Let me handle it. Go to your meeting and I'll see you after work."

"But what if you're some kind of criminal? And this is just your method of stealing cars?" Liza could hear the hysteria in her voice, but she didn't know how to calm down. This guy had wrecked her car, and now she was thinking about walking away from the accident and leaving him with her vehicle?

He smiled, and Liza felt her knees go weak. She leaned against the car. Gosh, he was handsome, and was that a dimple? *Be strong, Liza!* She couldn't just walk away from an accident. Isn't that what everyone said? Never leave the scene of the accident without calling the police. But her job was on the line. And this handsome stranger was offering to fix her car and let her drive his pickup to work.

She looked over at the white Ford pickup. Well, at least he had good taste. Her family was a Ford family. She sighed and took a closer look. The tires were brand-new and well-equipped for driving in Echo Ridge Canyon.

"My name is Jaime Maldonado. Here's my card with my number. Text me, and I'll update you on your car. You obviously know where I live, and no offense, but my pickup is a lot nicer than your car." He handed her the black electronic key fob. "Take it and be safe."

"I'm Liza Sorenson." She tucked the card in her pocket and curled her fingers around the key fob.

"It's nice to meet you, Liza, but I'm sorry we had to meet in this way," Jaime said.

She lifted her head, meeting his eyes. "Okay. I'm trusting you and I don't know why, but I guess it's because I don't have another option. I need this job."

Jaime pointed behind her. "I'm just going to jump in your car and back it up a little bit. No sense putting more scratches on my pickup."

Liza was going to reply with some sarcastic remark about him only caring about his pickup when she turned and saw the crumpled front end of her car. She shrugged. It was no use. She would think about it later. After her presentation. After she'd applied for the new position that her boss had been hinting about. She grabbed her bag and lunch sack out of the car, noticing that the stiffness in her neck had subsided. Hopefully, she could make it through the day.

She trudged through the snow and hopped into the heated leather seats of the pickup. The engine started up with the push of a button, and she searched for the defrost for a moment, then flipped it to high. She admired the display screen, which was larger than the one in her car. She changed the music from the local rock station to her favorite Christian music station and gripped the steering wheel. The leather was warm—the heated steering wheel was definitely a plus. After half a minute, she eased carefully out onto the highway and put the pickup into drive. Jaime waved to her as she drove away. She couldn't remember his last name. For a second, she questioned her sanity again. Maybe she'd hit her head in the accident. The responsible Liza would never leave her car broken down in some guy's driveway.

Wait, his business card would have a name on it. She fished it out of her pocket when she stopped at a red light. The card was printed in gray with black and white lettering. The design was simple, yet sleek and stylish. *Jaime Maldonado of Ratchet Revisions.* Underneath his name in script was printed, *Translation and editing services for your online business.*

She knew his name and his business now. She also knew that he was ruggedly handsome. No, he was gorgeous—more beautiful than should be humanly possible. He drove the nicest pickup she'd ever seen, and even though he'd wrecked her car, she would be seeing him again later that day. She told herself that the flutter in her stomach was because she was nervous about being late for her presentation. It didn't have anything to do with his caramel-colored skin, black hair, and green eyes.

Chapter Two

By the time Liza made it to the Stellar Ads parking lot, her trembling had nearly subsided, but she still felt on edge. Too much adrenaline coupled with the coffee she'd guzzled that morning had her nerves ready to explode.

She made herself take three cleansing breaths before she entered the office, then pasted a smile on her face and prepared to meet the wrath of Rick the Prick, as her coworkers liked to call him behind his back. Her mother would say that it was unladylike to even think of the moniker, but it suited her boss so well, she couldn't help it. Her smile turned genuine as she walked down the hallway toward the conference room. She was going to nail this presentation.

Nita, her best friend and coworker, met her at the

door, "Give us five minutes, Liza. Running just a tad slow this morning." Nita was the head of the design team, and she was always looking out for Liza. They had developed a good friendship over the past several months as they endured Rick's yo-yo personality, subtle threats, and firing rampages.

"No problem. See you soon." Inside Liza's head, she was doing backflips. She wouldn't have to hear Rick's disparaging comments about her being late or be threatened about her job. Phew. *Focus*, she reminded herself. She had everything set up in under five minutes, so when the rest of the team trailed in, Liza was ready. She didn't allow herself to think about her crumpled car, that handsome guy next door, or the fact that she had driven his pickup to work.

When Chrissy came in, Liza flashed her a smile despite the scowl Chrissy sent her way. She was one of the design team's underlings and resented the very breath in Liza's body. They had both applied for a new position last year, and when Liza was rewarded for her hard work, Chrissy took it personally. *Never mind,* Liza reminded herself. *I'm here to show them I deserve this.* Thankfully, her brain cooperated, and she was able to remember all of the major points of her presentation.

"Well done, Liza," Rick said as she finished. "You've done an excellent job of showing this team exactly what they need to do to make our clients happy. You also showed me you're the best candidate to attend the All-Star Design conference in Florida next week."

Liza froze. She started to open her mouth, closed it, and swallowed. She cleared her throat. "The All-Star Design conference?" Her voice squeaked. Anything but that. That was the design conference where she had first met Mark two years ago. Her ex-fiancé was a web designer, and they'd actually traveled to the conference together last year. She'd been engaged then. And this year, the creep would be there again with his company, a booth, and some floozy to try to attract male attention to his table space.

"Yes, you've been to that conference before and represented us well. I was undecided until I saw your presentation," Rick said. "But I'll get your name on that ticket today."

"But I wasn't planning on going, and I'm not sure I can get out of my prior engagement," Liza stuttered.

"Actually, she's quite adept at getting out of engagements," Chrissy mumbled at the same time Rick rolled back in his chair.

"I'm confident you'll make this work, Liza. I want you at that conference. Elaine, give her the details," Rick barked at his secretary. He turned back to the room and pointed at the door. "Let's get to work, folks."

Liza refused to look at Chrissy as they filed out of the conference room. She also refused to think of a certain word that best described her coworker.

Rick clapped her on the back at the end of the hall. "I see lots of good things happening for you, Liza. I'd like to meet with you tomorrow to discuss the action plan for gaining new clients at this conference."

"Sure, I'll get right on that. Thank you."

She walked back to her cubicle and flipped open her laptop. Her email chimed with an incoming message from Elaine with travel information for the All-Star Design conference.

"Noodles," Liza murmured as she opened the email. The All-Star Design Conference would be held in Orlando, Florida, on December sixth and seventh. The flights were already booked, leaving New York on Thursday the fifth and returning on Sunday.

"Psst, Liza, are you going to the conference?" Nita whispered as she slid around the corner of Liza's cubicle.

Liza jumped and swiveled in her chair. "Don't sneak up on me like that when I'm trying to think of an excuse to get out of going."

Nita sighed and sat on the edge of the desk. "They already booked your flights, didn't they?"

"Yes, it's not like I could get out of it anyway. I don't want to get fired."

"True," Nita replied. "Let's look on the bright side. Obviously, Rick thinks you're talented enough to go to the conference. Aren't you working on an application for a promotion?"

"Yeah, I don't know if anything will come of it. Rick

just keeps piling more work on me. I'll end up doing more work without being promoted."

"That stinks, but you don't. I'm so glad you work here. I wish I could go to the conference with you." Nita stood and put her hand on the back of Liza's chair. "Keep your chin up."

"Thanks, Nita." Liza lifted her chin and looked at the ceiling. "It looks like crunchy snow."

Nita laughed and tipped her head back too. "Crunchy, dirty snow. Guess I'd better get back to work."

"Thanks for the pep talk. I'm going so I'll make the best of it," Liza said. Nita patted her shoulder as she exited the cubicle.

Liza straightened and added the details of the conference to her calendar. When she decided to do something, she followed through with no more complaining and whining. Yep, she would make this work. The conference center would be enormous. It shouldn't be that hard to avoid Mark.

Her phone chirped with an incoming text.

Hey, sweets, I'm getting prepped for the big conference next week and thinking of you. Are you sure you don't want to come along with me? For old times' sake?

Liza's eyes widened and her heart drummed in her chest. The text was from Mark Pratt. She looked around her cubicle, as if she might find a video camera and studio crew filming her reaction. This couldn't be happening. Somehow, thinking of the no-good scoundrel had encouraged him to contact her again.

Almost ten months ago, Liza had been gearing up for a December wedding to Mark. They had dated for a year, and when he proposed on Valentine's Day, Liza felt so in love. She and her mom had planned the wedding, and Mark waited until after Liza had sold her apartment and moved in with her parents to call everything off. She'd already purchased a wedding gown and put down several nonrefundable deposits. Her parents had dipped into their savings to help her, and the catastrophe that followed was not something they could jump back from. Liza hadn't moved out on her own again. She lived with her parents and paid rent to help them make ends meet.

Liza deleted the text. Time to get back to work. She replied to Elaine and confirmed the details of the trip. As she sat back in her chair, she smiled as a new idea occurred to her. Maybe her mom could go with her on the trip. Her mother had just been complaining about the cold weather that morning, but if Liza could whisk her away to Florida, they could have some fun mother-daughter time in between the boring conference meetings. Liza knew it might be a long shot, but she asked Elaine for the cost breakdown to add a travel companion. Her mother could also act as a buffer between her and Mark. With that possibility on the horizon, Liza was able to get back to work and focus on her projects.

She was immersed in a new web design portfolio

when she remembered her car. Liza rubbed her forehead, wondering if maybe she had a little brain injury from the accident. How did someone forget something that important? Her mind immediately supplied the answers: the presentation, an invitation to a design conference she didn't want to attend, and the text from the creep.

Okay, so she had a lot on her mind. She dug out Jaime's business card and scanned the information again. Liza flipped the card over, but it was blank on the back. She wished there was a photo of Jaime included; she could use a little man candy to brighten her mood.

Liza slipped her feet out of her dress boots and curled her toes, popping them against the low pile carpet of her cubicle. Should she call him? Maybe just a text. Liza pulled out her phone and entered Jaime's contact information. Then she spent five minutes typing and deleting texts until she finally settled on the right one.

Hey, this is Liza Sorenson. I'm checking on the status of my car.

Liza hit send and was about to put her phone away and focus on her work when the phone chirped. She fumbled and almost dropped it in her eagerness to read the text.

Hi, Liza. Your car is in the shop. If they can't finish it today, you are welcome to use my pickup an extra day. Just stop by my house after work so I can get a few papers out of my pickup.

Liza pushed the autoresponder that said, **Okay,**

thanks. She couldn't afford to spend five more minutes on a simple text. Why was she agonizing over texting the guy who'd ruined her car in the first place? She'd heard something about his reputation; someone had said he liked to drink a little too much. No man was that good-looking. She was better off admiring his pickup.

Chapter Three

Jaime didn't like to take calls from his ex-wife, but Kori had baited him by texting to ask if she could call and talk about their son, Alex. Since Jaime would do anything for his fourteen-year-old boy, he'd agreed. That had been a mistake.

"Alex hates you and he doesn't want to be in boarding school," Kori spat.

"His teachers report that he's performing well and making lots of new friends," Jaime replied. "I suspect that is because he can finally take his medication on a regular basis."

"Are you blaming me for your son's disabilities?" Kori screeched.

"No, I'm saying that *our* son is doing well at school," Jaime replied evenly. "And I've asked you before to watch your tone when discussing Alex's disabilities."

For the past three years, Jaime had tried unsuccessfully to monitor Alex's medication schedule for his severe ADHD. The medication disappeared on a regular basis, and when he'd discovered that Kori had been taking their son's prescription drugs, he'd confronted her. She'd denied ever taking them, but when Jaime gave her an ultimatum—allow Alex to attend boarding school or have Kori submit to drug testing—she'd relented. She had turned into a bitter and angry woman without her supply of drugs. The divorce was finalized right before Alex enrolled in his first year of boarding school. Now he was in his second year and doing remarkably well.

Kori began a tirade of cuss words and creative names. Jaime gripped the phone and held it away from his ear as his ex-wife screamed at him: "You're the most irresponsible, worthless excuse for a father I know!"

"And yet I'm the only father Alex has, and I'm going to be there for him." Jaime caught himself pacing in front of the large picture window of the family room. It was almost five thirty, so Liza would arrive soon and he had to keep things cool. If Kori found out about his accident, her current tirade would look like a fluffy kitten party. He couldn't believe how lucky he'd been—well, first he was stupid because he wasn't paying attention and got in a wreck. If Liza had called the cops, it would ruin everything. But she hadn't.

The beautiful brunette had been so worried about her work presentation that she'd agreed to rush off to work in his pickup. Because of that, Jaime had been praying his thanks all day. He had made a promise to the Lord that he would do right by his son, but it had been much more difficult to keep that promise than Jaime could have imagined.

"How do I know you aren't drinking again?" Kori demanded, bringing his attention back to the conversation.

"How do I know you haven't found another source of stimulants to get you through the day?"

"I should call the cops on you right now," she said.

"I have work to do, Kori. If you need something, send me an email. And before you threaten me again, remember that the cops will want to know my side of the story, too." Jaime ended the call before Kori could say anything else. His crazy ex-wife was determined to bring him down, and she didn't care if it hurt Alex. That was one of the reasons he protected Alex at all costs.

Jaime looked out the window again and then walked back into the kitchen. No sense having Liza catch him gawking out the window like some kind of stalker. If only he'd been paying better attention this morning, then he wouldn't be so stressed out that he couldn't concentrate on his work. He frowned, knowing that his real problems were his actions from six months ago. He glanced at the family Bible near the arm of the sofa. Walking forward with faith was the only thing he could do right lately, and he wasn't ready to give up yet.

A knock on the door interrupted his musings. Jaime walked quickly, reminding himself to stay calm. He opened the door, and all thoughts of calm fled. Liza wore a puffy pink coat that matched the color of her cheeks. Her hair was braided to the side, and her dark eyes sparkled with a hint of her vibrant character. Had Liza been this beautiful that morning?

"Hi, Liza. Let me just slip on my boots and I'll come get that stuff out of the pickup. Thanks for stopping by." His words came out in a rush. So much for playing it cool.

"No problem." She brushed a strand of hair behind her ear. "Thanks for getting my car fixed. I'm still a little worried that we didn't call the cops and report the incident. My dad is going to ask me why I didn't do that."

"What's there to worry about?" Jaime pulled the front door closed and headed down the steps. She couldn't call the cops. He couldn't let a little fender bender be the end of his hope to save Alex from his crazy mother. "I told you I'd fix your car, and it will be delivered to you better than it was. How did your presentation go?"

Liza's face registered a moment of surprise, and then she brightened. "Actually, it went really well. I was afraid I was going to bomb because of all the adrenaline, but my boss was impressed."

"I'm glad to hear it." Jaime breathed an inward sigh of relief at the quick change in subject. "Where do you work?"

"Stellar Ads. I'm one of their editors, and I create lots of ad copy."

Jaime reached into his pickup and grabbed a stack of papers and envelopes out of the console. "That's cool. We work in similar fields."

"Yeah, I noticed that from your card." Liza slipped her hands into her coat pockets.

That simple movement seemed so graceful. The way she carried herself with an air of quiet confidence left him wanting to know more about her. He stuffed the stack of papers under his arm, trying to think of what to say.

"Do you work from home?" Liza asked before he could come up with a witty remark.

Jaime nodded. "I do. Cuts down on overhead. Maybe one day I'll go back to an office, but the view here is pretty great."

She turned and looked past his house. "It *is* beautiful here. I always admire your property when I drive by."

"Thanks. So you just live north of here? I think I met your dad when I first moved in. Reuben, right?"

"Yes, that's my dad. I live with my parents." She looked down at the ground. "Wish I could say I worked from home. I work in a cubicle, and trust me, there's no view."

Jaime chuckled. "Yeah, I did my time in the cubicles. Never want to go back."

When she lifted her head, she was smiling and her

brown eyes sparkled. "Sometime you'll have to tell me how you escaped the cubicles."

Jaime kicked some snow off the tire with his boot. "Escape is definitely the right word. I'll update you about your car tomorrow. They wanted to finish sooner, but they were waiting on a part. I'm really sorry about the inconvenience."

Liza nodded. "It's okay. I'm glad it turned out all right. I'll see you tomorrow."

He watched as she climbed into his pickup and drove off. Looking up at the sky, Jaime noticed more swollen clouds packed with snow. It was supposed to drop another two inches on Echo Ridge tonight.

Nights like these were perfect for cozying up in front of the warm fire, yet they still made Jaime feel a pang of loneliness. He didn't miss Kori and he would never go back to her, but he missed Alex. It had been a little over a year since the divorce, and Jaime had worked hard to get Alex into a boarding school and away from Kori. Unfortunately, that boarding school took Alex away from him as well. Jaime told himself that it was worth it, but sometimes he wondered if he had made the right choice. He wanted shared custody of his son—not just the standard every other weekend he'd been assigned, but because of the mistakes he'd made he had a lot of work to do to put together a good case.

Jaime headed back inside, removed his boots, and began building a fire. His thoughts returned to Liza

Sorensen. She was young, beautiful, and vivacious, and he realized that she didn't seem afraid of him. Echo Ridge was a small town, so gossip had a way of traveling quickly whether a person wanted it to or not. Six months ago, during a very low time in his life, Jaime had drunk way more than he should have and then tried to drive himself home. The result was a broken fence and an arrest for a misdemeanor offense—driving under the influence. The cops had warned him that he wouldn't get a second chance. If he made any more trouble in Echo Ridge, he would be charged with a felony.

He'd done really well to keep his nose clean until today. He'd awakened at three o'clock. He couldn't get back to sleep and finally got up and worked for a couple hours. At six o'clock, the tendonitis in his wrist was killing him, so he'd downed a couple shots of vodka and fallen back asleep until seven-thirty. He'd been headed over to Fay's Café for morning coffee when he'd pulled out in front of Liza. In a panic, he'd realized that even though he was clearheaded, he might still fail the breathalyzer test. He could be arrested and charged as a felon. And then what? He didn't want to know what, so he did the only thing he could: bypass the cops and pay to fix Liza's car himself.

Jaime rarely drank since the night of his DUI, and he'd never been one for getting drunk anyway, but he'd let his weaknesses conquer him that night. If anything, the events of that night had solidified his desire to do better and be better. He'd stayed married too long when he should've left and taken Alex with him. By the time he'd finally left, it was too late. Kori had wreaked such havoc on their lives that Jaime couldn't undo the damage. Kori had convinced their son to hate him, but Jaime held out hope that one day Alex would be mature enough to make his own opinions about his dad. In the meantime, Jaime would pray and try to make up the difference.

He was angry at himself for being weak that morning and going back to the bottle that had started his problems. Stomping through the kitchen, he yanked open the cupboard under the sink, pulled out the bottle of vodka, dumped it down the drain, and threw it in the trash. There. He was done drinking. No more excuses, and no more foolishness. Alex needed him, and Jaime was ready to be the father he should have been all along.

Chapter Four

As Liza drove away from Jaime's house, her smile widened. She meant every word she had said to Jaime. She was looking forward to seeing him tomorrow, but it had nothing to do with her car. Her parents' home was less than five minutes from Jaime's house and she was still thinking about him when she pulled into the driveway. She hummed to herself as she walked into her parents' kitchen.

"Sounds like someone had a good day," her mom said by way of greeting. Adina Sorenson was slight in stature, yet a little thick around the middle. She didn't look the part of a fifth-grade teacher with her silver hair in a long French braid, but she was one of the most requested teachers at Echo Ridge Elementary.

"Yep, it was quite the day." Liza hugged her mom, her

nose twitching at the familiar scent of her vanilla perfume.

"Did your presentation go well?"

"It was great." Liza snitched a roll from the basket on the counter. "The only downside is that my boss was so impressed, he invited me to attend the All-Star Design conference in Florida next week."

Mom stepped back and raised her eyebrows. "Isn't that the same conference—"

"That I went to with Mark last year? Yes, and that's why I'm hoping you can come with me." Liza took a bite of the roll and closed her eyes briefly as the tender flavor divided her attention. "Yummy. Mom, your rolls are the best. Can you come? I fly out next Thursday."

"Liza, I would love to, but Sharla took a turn for the worse." Mom rubbed her forehead and sighed. "They don't think she'll last the week."

Liza gasped. "So soon? But I thought Sharla was doing better." Her mother's best friend, Marianne, had moved to Echo Ridge to help take care of her sister, Sharla, in her battle against cancer.

"I know. She's fought this fight so hard, but Marianne said that hospice has taken over care. I don't dare leave because Marianne will need me for the funeral."

"That makes me feel bad for Marianne and her sister." Liza filled up a glass of water and drank it in three gulps.

"I know, but at least Marianne has had three years to prepare. No one thought Sharla would live this long." She scrubbed a few potatoes in the sink as she spoke. "Will you be okay? Will *he* be there?"

"Yes, and yes," Liza answered. "It's a huge conference. I probably won't even run into him." She made sure that her voice sounded upbeat and optimistic. No sense in creating more stress for her mom. Liza would have to make sure that she stayed out of Mark's sight—a feat that would be nearly impossible because Mark had already texted her about the conference.

Liza helped her mom finish up dinner preparation. Her dad worked for the post office, and there were always plenty of opportunities for overtime during the holiday season. They planned dinner for seven o'clock, so while the chicken was roasting, Liza rode her exercise bike and tried to sort out everything that happened that day. She hadn't mentioned the creep's text to her mother, because it would only upset her more. She also hadn't mentioned her fender bender, because she was worried that her mom might call the cops right then. Better to wait until her dad came home. Reuben Sorenson was as levelheaded as they came.

Liza cleaned up and headed out to the kitchen just before seven to make sure she was around when her dad arrived. Her mom hadn't noticed the pickup out front because she went into her office to grade papers after Liza finished helping her with dinner.

"Who's here?" Her dad asked as he came into the kitchen.

"Just us, dear," Mom answered.

"But there's a fancy ride out front, and it ain't mine." Dad jerked his thumb behind him towards the driveway.

That was Liza's cue. "I drove that home, and there's a pretty good story behind it."

"Oh?" Dad raised his eyebrows in a move similar to Mom's earlier.

Liza chuckled. "Let's sit down and start eating, and I'll explain everything." It took her a few minutes to describe the accident, and a few more minutes to describe why she had left the scene of an accident and gone to work.

"Liza, you need to call the insurance company," Mom said. "Who did you say ran into you?"

"Well, technically I ran into him." Liza held up her hand. "It was the guy next door. Jaime Maldonado. But he's fixing my car."

"He is?" Dad asked. "I thought he did work online. Is he a mechanic?"

Liza laughed. "No, Dad. He took my car to the shop, and they're fixing it."

Dad took another bite of chicken and chewed slowly. "Well, he seems like a trustworthy guy. It should be okay as long as there are no problems with your car. I'll want to check it out when it comes back," Dad said in his no-nonsense voice.

"I'd planned on it."

"I thought I heard he had a little drinking problem," Mom said. "I'm not sure if he's as trustworthy as he acts."

"Well, that's neither here nor there, because we just don't know," Dad replied. "He seemed like a stand-up guy when I met him."

"I didn't smell any alcohol on him," Liza said.

"Well, just be careful," Mom told her. "You never know."

Liza ate the last bite of chicken from her plate. "Thanks for dinner, Mom."

"Thank you for helping me prepare it as usual. Liza, it's been so nice having you here with us. I know this isn't exactly how you wanted things to turn out, but I hope you're happy."

Liza sucked in a breath and smiled. "I am happy. I love Echo Ridge. I keep making plans for my life, but there's always some plot twist I didn't expect, so I'm trying to roll with it."

Dad chuckled. "Now there's the writer we know and love."

"Are you finding any time to work on your writing?" Mom asked.

"Not as much as I would like, but maybe there will be time in Orlando."

"Orlando?" Dad asked

Liza spent the next few minutes explaining the conference to her dad and reassuring him that she would not run into Mark. After they cleaned up the kitchen, she went to her room and sat on her bed with her laptop. For as long as she could remember, she had wanted to be a writer. By definition, her job was writing, but she wanted to write novels. She'd been working on a new novel—a romance—when she was engaged to Mark. After he broke her heart, she couldn't find her voice, and the characters just seemed to want to cry as much as she did. In frustration and heartbreak, she had shelved that book and immersed herself in work at Stellar Ads. It had been almost a year since then, and she was just starting to feel the stirrings of a story again.

She flexed her fingers and grinned. It had been too long. Definitely time to turn over a new page in her life. Liza started typing out notes, and for some reason the main character looked a lot like Jaime: incredibly handsome with a skin tone that hinted at Latin descent, but where did his striking green eyes come from? There had been something in Jaime's speech that hinted at an accent from a language other than Spanish or English. Something melodic. She would have to investigate that further.

Liza shook her head. She was already planning on talking to Jaime more, but maybe she wouldn't even see him tomorrow. Maybe he'd just drop off her car and take his pickup home. Oh well, at least he had inspired her. It was always hardest for her to picture her main characters in detail. She loved getting inspiration from real-life people and mixing and matching characteristics to create the hero or heroine. She couldn't be sure, but she thought she'd seen a dimple in Jaime's left cheek today. That was another fun detail to add to the character she was creating.

Liza wrote down some notes and a few phrases in the file before closing up her laptop. It was hard to concentrate with the All-Star Design conference coming up. Her mother would've been the perfect buffer against Mark, but now what could she do?

Mark had called off her wedding because he'd cheated on her and "fallen in love" with the flavor of the month. About six months ago, he had called her up to apologize. He told her that he was a changed man and begged for another chance. Liza still remembered the moment with clarity. She'd felt her heart softening toward the man that she had once loved—and then, with a snap, reality had whacked her upside the head and she'd hung up on him, vowing never to speak to him again. But Mark wasn't easily dissuaded. He'd sent her flowers, letters, emails, and texts and even dropped by her home and work. When Liza threatened to call the police, he backed off. She hadn't heard from him in about two months. Her hope was that he had moved on, but this morning's text proved that wasn't the case.

Liza groaned and put a pillow over her head as she sank deeper into the comforter. If only there was someone who would pretend to be her boyfriend. Liza moved the pillow and pushed the hair from her eyes.

Nope, that wouldn't work either. Mark had proven that a boyfriend wasn't any threat to him; if anything, it made him more tenacious. When he had decided to pursue Liza again, she accepted several dates with a nerdy guy—who mumbled a lot and spilled his food down the front of his shirt on every date—in the hopes that it would deter Mark. Unfortunately, it didn't work, even though she'd sent pictures of them together in reply to his texts. No, she'd have to think of something stronger than a boyfriend. Maybe a restraining order? She smiled. Now that would be a story.

With a yawn, Liza decided to head to bed early. She would have to leave even earlier in the morning for work, because another storm was brewing and it would definitely let loose in Echo Ridge Canyon.

Chapter Five

"Liza, glad you made it on time." Rick clapped his hands as Liza entered his office the next morning. "I'm so glad you decided to get smart about this conference. I just got off the phone with Mark Pratt, and he will be there and wants you to take a look at his client roster."

Liza gaped at her boss. "That isn't funny, Rick." She sat down in the office chair and set her laptop on the table. Rick knew all about her broken engagement to Mark, but why would he tease her?

"I'm not trying to be funny," Rick replied. "I'm serious. Look, I know he's your ex, but his business is booming—"

"No. His business is booming because he's a criminal. He rips off anybody who comes into contact with him." Liza straightened, closed her eyes, let out a breath, and opened her eyes again. "Do you want to keep your business?" She leveled a glare at Rick.

"Whoa, where is this all coming from?"

Liza swallowed. She was definitely pushing the boundary with Rick in a way that she never had before, but how could he be so callous and brainless? "This is coming from my ex being a manipulative, degrading, destructive thief. I don't want to ever talk to him again."

"Well, that's too bad. Your name is on the ticket. You're attending the conference, and I set up a meeting with him." Rick folded his arms.

Liza leaned forward and put her head in her hand. "You realize that Mark only set up a meeting so that he could talk to me? You're not going to get any new business from this."

"I don't believe that's the case. Liza, how much do you value your job?"

And there it was. Rick the Prick was threatening to fire her if she didn't have a meeting with her emotionally abusive ex-fiancé. For half a second, Liza thought about quitting. Actually, she thought about spitting in Rick's face. But she couldn't do either. She wasn't paying very much rent to her parents, but it was enough to keep them afloat. They were trying desperately to pay off some medical bills from last year and recover from the expenses of the wedding that didn't happen.

That was the only reason that Liza gritted her teeth, turned toward Rick, and said, "I value my job and I enjoy working here. I do not want to talk to Mark Pratt, because he hinders my ability to do a good job. I have scanned the list of attendees at the conference and already set up appointments of my own. There are so many people there who I'm better qualified to speak with."

"Well, we'll just have to rearrange your schedule so you can fit in another meeting with Mark." Rick leaned forward and his gut pushed out onto the table. "I'm not negotiating here. You're going to the conference and you'll do what needs to be done."

Liza heard "or else" without him speaking it. She seethed inside, imagining herself as a giant volcano with lava boiling and frothing at the edges. At least she wouldn't have to think very hard about the characteristics of the villain in her new novel. "Fine. I understand that you're threatening my job if I don't speak to someone who I am uncomfortable with."

"Well, no. I'm just asking you to do your job. This happens to be the job description."

Liza kept her mouth in a thin line, enjoying that Rick was backtracking a little. He would get his comeuppance, but it wouldn't be soon enough. "You have threatened me. But I need this job, so I'll go."

She picked up her laptop and headed out the door. As soon as she could spare a moment, she would start looking for a new job. For now, she was still locked into this one, and somehow her worst nightmare had come true. Not only did she have to be in the same room as Mark, but she would have to endure a meeting with him as well.

Liza went to the ladies' restroom to compose herself before anyone saw her angry tears. Ten deep breaths in a row helped her to calm down, and she decided that she would think about Rick, Mark, and the ensuing meeting later. It was making her sick with worry to consider it now.

She ended up being swamped for the rest of the day. Between last-minute edits on several of the new website designs and time spent prepping for the conference, the day sped by.

Jaime texted her just after two o'clock to let her know that her car was ready and she could pick it up at his place. She had to bite back a grin, because it meant that she would get to see him again. Even as she smiled, she warned herself to stop it. She didn't know anything about him, aside from the rumors that he might have a drinking problem. Her mental warnings did nothing to calm the butterflies in her stomach, though, and she smiled as she thought about how she might write about Jaime that night in her novel.

"I know that smile," Nita said as she passed her cubicle.

"What smile?" Liza replied innocently.

"Men are trouble, Liza. Trouble with a capital T."

"Who said anything about men? I'm not dating anyone."

Nita leaned against the cubicle wall. "But you're thinking pretty hard about someone, and that spells trouble."

Liza laughed. "Just daydreaming about the hero for my new book."

Nita stepped inside and sat on the edge of Liza's desk. "Wait, you're writing again?"

"I think so." Liza shrugged.

"You have real talent. Don't let life keep you from pursuing your dreams." Nita tapped her fingers on the desk. "So who is the guy?"

"Oh, just a guy I got in a fender bender with yesterday. He's fixing my car, and he let me drive his pickup to work."

"Wait. What?" Nita gasped. "You got in a wreck yesterday and didn't tell me?"

"No time, but I'll tell you the abbreviated version now." Liza shared the high and low points of her morning with Nita, ending with Jaime texting her to say that her car was now finished.

Nita shook her head. "You. Did. Not. Tell me you didn't agree not to call the cops or your insurance company?"

Liza pressed her teeth into her bottom lip and looked upward. "Maybe. Look, before you say anything, he's the guy next door. My parents know him. I couldn't miss my presentation."

"Well, he'd better do a pretty sweet job on fixing your car, because that's breaking all kinds of laws."

"It's not breaking laws, Nita. It didn't do very much damage to my car, and he got it fixed. Honestly, I didn't want to call the insurance either, because I can't risk mine going up."

"Well, it wouldn't, because it wasn't your fault. But whatever. Just be careful." Nita drummed her fingers on the desk again. "What's his motivation for not calling the cops?"

"He was just helping me. He could see I was totally stressed out about missing my presentation."

Nita tilted her head to the right and narrowed her eyes. "You really think so?"

"Yeah, why else?"

"That's the question you should be asking." Nita patted her on the shoulder and clicked her tongue. "Trouble. Men are trouble."

Liza told herself that she agreed, but by the time the workday ended, she was looking forward to seeing Jaime again. Just to double-check if he really did have a dimple in his left cheek. That was all. Oh, and to stop by his house and drop off his pickup.

As she neared the base of Echo Ridge Canyon and the wide arc in the road that brought her to Jaime's property, Liza found herself gripping the steering wheel a bit too hard. She pulled into his driveway slowly, cut the engine, and hopped out. The snow from that morning had dropped about three new inches on Echo Ridge, and his property reminded her of a Christmas movie. The white paneling with green shutters just needed a few red bows and it could be featured on a Christmas card. The snow was scraped clean from all the walks and piled along the edges. Her car sat in the driveway, and she traced her fingers along the Ford Fusion emblem. The headlight had been replaced, as had the front bumper. Her car looked like it hadn't suffered a wreck at all.

Liza climbed the front steps, relieved to be getting her car back. She knocked on the beautiful hardwood door, wondering at the sudden flutter in her stomach. She heard steps approaching and commanded her nerves to be still as the door swung open.

"Liza, it's good to see you. Why don't you come in for a moment? I have receipts and paperwork detailing the repairs on your car." Jaime stepped aside and motioned for her to follow him.

"Oh, okay. I'm glad everything is done. My car looks like it did a couple days ago before our run-in."

"Maybe even a tiny bit better. The guys at the shop spruced it up nicely," Jaime said as he walked through the house.

She followed him into the great room and kitchen area, surveying the dark cherrywood cabinets and dark gray countertops. The custom home wasn't what most people would expect for a bachelor. Jaime's business must be quite successful. "Your home is beautiful."

"Thank you. I can't really take credit—this is one of Billy Redford's homes."

"He does excellent work. I thought you weren't from Echo Ridge. Do you know him?"

"We know each other from our college days. He made sure I knew how to find my way in this little town." Jaime looked past Liza toward the backyard covered in snow. "It's really grown on me these past six months."

"That's good to hear. Some city people can't handle the slower pace of life." Liza watched him to see his reaction. Was he more of a city boy or a country boy?

"Not me. I was raised outside Buffalo, and I prefer the quieter scene."

"I guess that's why we both work behind computers, eh?"

"Yep." He grinned, and a dimple appeared in his left cheek.

Liza's tummy tingled as she smiled back.

Jaime handed her a stack of papers and receipts. "I clipped all the information together here. If you have any problems, let me know."

"As long as it runs well, there shouldn't be a problem. I couldn't see a scratch out there." Liza took the papers and tried not to notice the way her fingers buzzed as his strong hands brushed against hers.

"Hey, I really owe you one," Jaime said. "I appreciate

you trusting me and saving me from a huge headache with the police and my insurance. I like my insurance rates; I wasn't looking for them to be raised."

"Yeah, that's what my friend was telling me today. You do owe me one. But one what?"

Jaime smiled. "Dinner?"

"That might be nice, but really, I'm just grateful for my car." Liza smiled at him. He was so handsome. Why wasn't she jumping for the chance to go out to dinner with him? She could just hear Nita scolding her now about missing out on the perfect opportunity to date.

"I need to do something for you, though." He rubbed the bit of scruff on his chin.

Liza was struck with an idea. A wild, crazy, totally insane idea. Her stomach had been tied up in knots all day as she'd considered how she could get out of meeting with Mark. There were no job openings in Echo Ridge, and she wasn't looking to relocate, so for now, she had to keep working at Stellar Ads with Rick the Prick. With this burst of inspiration, though, she could turn the tables.

"Wait a minute," Jaime said. "Something's going on. You should've seen your face just now. What's your idea?"

Liza grinned. She'd never been good at playing poker. "I just got the best idea. I don't need dinner. I need some help. My boss is a real jerk, and today he set up a meeting with me and my ex-fiancé and then threatened me with my job if I didn't go through with it."

"Whoa, that's borderline harassment. He can't do that to you."

"He did. And he does all the time. He loves threatening people with their jobs. We have a nickname for him at work, but I can't say it. His name is Rick, so I'll let you use your imagination."

Jaime thought about it for two seconds and then burst out laughing. "I got it. So how can I help you? And you were engaged?"

"Yes. It was almost a year ago. My ex cheated on me, and then he decided he wanted me back. He's been crazy ever since." Liza's voice trembled and she spoke softly, trying to hide her anxiety.

"I'm really sorry to hear that you had to go through that," Jaime said.

Liza nodded. "It's better now. I wanted to take my mom to the conference with me, but she can't make it."

"You're not talking about the All-Star Design conference, are you?" Jaime leaned forward. "I was thinking about going."

"No way." Liza straightened, hoping she'd heard him right.

"Way." Jaime grinned. "I think I see where this is heading. You want me to pretend to be your boyfriend?"

"Oh no," Liza replied. She hesitated for half a second before blurting out, "I want you to be my fake fiancé."

Chapter Six

Jaime stepped back and rubbed his ear. "I must not have heard correctly. Did you just ask me to pretend to be your fiancé?"

"I know it sounds crazy, but it's just for one weekend. If you'll just go to the conference with me and pretend to be my fiancé, you never have to speak to me again when we get back." Liza gave him one of the best puppy-dog looks he'd ever seen.

"How about we start with a date? I'm sure we can come up with some way to keep you away from your ex. Who is this guy, anyway?"

"Mark Pratt." The way Liza said his name, you would think she was spitting out poison. "He's a web designer, and he'll have a booth there."

Jaime leaned back against the kitchen counter. "I

know that name. That guy's a jerk, and he stole a bunch of my clients!" Mark had come to him wanting help with translation services and then ended up skimming some of his clients in the process. Jaime studied Liza. A moment ago her idea sounded crazy, but now he understood why she didn't want to speak with Mark.

"See? You can help me. Besides, this conference is in your field. It would be an excellent place to hand out business cards and pick up more clients." Liza put her hand on his arm. "It will be more like a date. We don't have to tell anyone. Except Mark. He is the only one we need to tell. To everyone else, we can just look like we're friends."

She did have a point. The conference was in Florida, and no one from Echo Ridge or his former life would likely be there. If anyone saw them together, it wouldn't be painful to claim the beautiful brunette as his date. At the very least, they could be friendly colleagues. But Mark Pratt was the ultimate creep. "I don't know about coming into contact with Mark again. Last time he lost me a bunch of business."

"So here's your chance to get back at him and build your business at the same time," Liza replied. "We can help each other."

Jaime rubbed the back of his neck. His business was doing well, but he wanted the opportunity to expand. "Just for the weekend? No one else knows?"

"Yep."

Jaime hesitated. He was about to do something crazy, but it felt like the right thing to do. He held out his hand. "Deal."

Liza shook his hand with vigor. "Deal. And since you were thinking about asking me out anyway, it all works out." She winked.

A laugh erupted from Jaime's middle, surprising him. Liza started laughing too. She leaned against the counter, right next to him. He could smell coconut in her hair and barely resisted the urge to tuck the hair behind her ear as she turned to him with a bright smile. "You're funny," he said. "When I said I owed you one, this isn't exactly what I had in mind, but we'll make it work."

"Let's see if we can get the same flight. When I looked at the flight, there were several empty seats left."

He liked this woman. She knew how to take charge of a situation. He wouldn't describe her as bossy, though, more confident and direct. "What about a ring?"

Liza looked down at her left hand. "Oh yeah. Hmm, I'll look through my jewelry. I'm sure I can find something that can play the part for the weekend."

They chatted while Liza found the airline and flight and helped Jaime book his tickets. He was able to get a seat right next to hers. Agreeing to do this was crazy, but he couldn't ignore the attraction he felt toward Liza. He wanted to get to know her better. This might be an unorthodox way to do it, but it would be much faster than if he'd just asked her on a date.

"You know we're going to have to do some studying in order to pull this off," Jaime said.

"Is it that far-fetched?" Liza twisted her watch around her wrist. When she looked at him, he could see a line of gold around her pupil. Her eyes were beautiful—she was beautiful.

He mentally shook himself. "No, but considering our new arrangement, I think it'd be wise to spend a little time together so that we can get Mark to believe it. He may be a scumbag, but he's smart."

Liza nodded. "So are you asking me on a date?"

Jaime laughed. "Yeah, it's a little weird asking you on a date after agreeing to be your fiancé, but I think that's what I'm doing." He put his hand to the side of his mouth and whispered, "It's a business meeting, but we'll call it a date when we're undercover."

Liza playfully pushed his shoulder. "Well, you should know my favorite food is pizza from Jack's Pizza Shack."

Jaime's mouth watered at the mere mention of the downtown restaurant. "Jack's is the best. How about tomorrow? The Saturday crowd is busy, so could I pick you up at six?"

"I think that sounds great." Liza stood up straight and rolled her shoulders back. "I'll jot down some talking points that we can bring up during the meeting with

Mark. We'll make sure we have background information on each other to pull off this façade."

"See you tomorrow, then."

After Liza left in her car, Jaime went in the bathroom and scrubbed his face with cold water. He still couldn't believe it. Had he actually agreed to be his neighbor's fake fiancé? Liza's reassurance made it sound like an innocent favor, but he couldn't help feeling like they were playing a dangerous game. He was attracted to her, and she had been flirting with him. What if they discovered they really liked each other?

The ringing of his phone pulled him from his thoughts. Jaime smiled when he saw his son's face on the screen. He'd been trying to reach Alex for nearly a week and finally his son was calling him back. "Hi Alex," Jaime said.

"Dad, I need to know why you won't help Mom pay her bills." Alex's voice was terse.

Jaime paused and pushed a hand through his hair. "Son, I've gone over this with you before. I'm following the divorce decree and I've given your mother extra to—"

"She said that you would say that. It's a lie!" Alex shouted. "You abandoned us and you just want to punish her. That's why you sent me to this school!"

"Alex, I love you, that is why I worked so hard to get you into that school. Your mother shouldn't be discussing these things with you. What is it that you need?" Jaime tried to steer away from the fight and keep his voice calm. Already his neck felt flushed with anger at his ex-wife and the lengths she was willing to go to.

"I already told you. My teacher suggested some books to go along with the course and I need some new gym shorts." Alex sighed as if he were talking to a small child.

Jaime clenched his fist. "I sent your mother an extra hundred dollars to cover those expenses."

"No, you didn't," Alex said. "She doesn't even have enough money to buy groceries for the rest of the month."

"From now on, if you need something, I will purchase it for you and make sure you receive it. Please send me an exact list of what you need and I'll make sure it's ordered and on its way to your school."

"So you think you can buy my love?" Alex spat. "You think you can just go find some girlfriend to replace Mom and make you feel better about yourself?"

Jamie barely swallowed back the growl forming in the back of his throat. "I love you no matter how much you hate me. I will love you forever, no matter what you do. I won't ever stop loving you because you are my son."

"Yeah, right," Alex said and ended the call.

Jaime sunk onto the edge of his bed and rubbed his forehead, a deep sigh pushing its way from his chest. Alex's comment about Jaime replacing his mother reeked of Kori. His phone pinged a minute later with the details of the supplies Alex needed. Jaime's chest felt tight as he scrolled through the details and ordered what Alex needed. He wouldn't make the same mistake again. From now on, Kori wouldn't get an extra cent from him under the guise of providing for their son.

Jaime wandered into the kitchen and pulled a Diet Coke from the fridge. He poured it over ice and drank it slowly, ignoring the old craving for something stronger to cover his pain. It was time for things to change in his life for good. Liza was a reminder that he didn't have to go back to the old way of life.

His phone pinged with an incoming message and he groaned. When he saw that it was from Kori, he almost ignored it. Instead, he counted to five, disengaged from the moment, and then opened the text. It had taken a lot of practice to get to this point. Kori had a way of getting under his skin. Most likely Alex had called her right after hanging up with him and she had done her best to poison him and hide the truth.

You don't have a chance of gaining custody of Alex. He needs a mother. You're not even dating anyone.

Jaime thought a moment before replying. Usually, he just ignored Kori's messages. But today was different.

How would you know? And I agree, Alex does need a mother.

He smiled when he hit send, but Kori had a good point. The courts were reluctant to allow fathers more than fifty percent custody of their kids, and even more so if there wasn't a stable home for them to live in. He'd heard of people faking relationships and even marriages in order to win custody battles, but that seemed a little far-fetched. For now, he just wanted to concentrate on what he could do—and that was work hard and keep Alex in school and away from his crazy mother.

Chapter Seven

Liza hadn't been this excited in months. Jaime would pick her up in half an hour, and they were going on a date. Yes, she knew it was really just a business meeting, but it felt more like a date. Jaime was willing to take her out in Echo Ridge, which meant that he probably liked her. The fact that he had agreed to be her fake fiancé left her wondering how much was due to her charm and how much was due to him owing her a favor. What if Nita was right? Maybe he did have good reason not to get the police involved in the accident because of some nefarious background.

After Mark had broken off their engagement, she'd steered clear of men for nearly six months. Then, with urging from friends like Nita and her parents, she'd started dating again. It was a scary adventure. She'd gone on dates here and there, but pretty much all of them first dates—the kind where she tried to decide how much to share of herself, while at the same time gently digging to find out whether the guy was a serial killer. Disappointing wasn't a strong enough word to describe dating after a major breakup. Devastating. Diabolical. Discouraging. Dejected. Yeah, those were better descriptors.

Liza shoved her worries aside. Whatever the case, she was going out with one of the most gorgeous guys in Echo Ridge, and she could almost taste the barbecue chicken pizza dotted with fresh pieces of pineapple—a Jack's Pizza Shack specialty. She zipped up her favorite pair of black boots over skinny jeans. She also wore a white sweater with silver threading, and she had curled her hair into soft brown waves falling over her shoulder.

"Knock, knock." Her mom rapped on the open door. "You look beautiful, dear. It's about time you went on another date."

"Thanks, Mom. But this is more of a business meeting. Jaime and I are discussing options for his company." Liza stuffed her lip gloss in her purse and tried to act nonchalant.

"Well, the sparkle in your eyes says otherwise. Be careful. Jaime seems like a nice guy, but I've heard a little more than I can ignore."

Liza looked up at the note of concern in her mother's voice. "What exactly have you heard?"

Her mom leaned against the dresser. "I'm fairly

certain he got picked up for a DUI shortly after moving to Echo Ridge."

Liza pressed her lips together and looked at the floor. That was much worse than a rumor about someone drinking a bit too much. "Really? Do you believe that, Mom? I want your honest opinion."

"I'm not sure, but I do know that people make mistakes, and sometimes they are big mistakes. I've heard that he pretty much keeps to himself, but still ..." She smoothed a stray hair away from Liza's face. "Pay attention to how much he drinks."

"I will. I've heard a few rumors too." Jaime didn't seem like the drinking type, but she would find out tonight. Although phrasing the question *So have you been arrested for a DUI?* might prove more difficult than she imagined. "Okay, I'm almost ready. Wish me luck." Even though she'd told her mother it was a business date, she couldn't ignore the flutter in her stomach as she walked out into the front room.

Dad turned the television off and stood, brushing a few crumbs off his shirt. "Hot date tonight, then?"

"No, it's a business meeting." Liza stood in front of her dad and wiped a few more crumbs off his shirt. "Hey, Dad, can we skip the doorstep scene?"

He stepped back and held up his hands with a chuckle. "Sure, but if there's another 'business meeting'—" He put his fingers in the air as if putting quotes around the words. "—you'll have to let me chat with him."

"Thanks, Dad." Liza kissed him on the cheek. She stepped toward the window and saw headlights shining up the drive. "I'll see you guys later." She pulled her leather jacket off the hook. The maroon color looked great with her white sweater and she wondered if Jaime would notice. *Stop it*, she commanded herself. This was only a business meeting—at least that's what she had planned on, even if Jaime was too attractive for his own good. She tried to remind herself that it was only a means to an end: getting Mark to leave her alone. After the conference, she'd come back, get to work, and forget about Jaime and their fake engagement. That was why she didn't plan on telling her parents about their crazy plan. No sense getting them worked up over a weekend scheme.

Liza opened the door and hurried down the steps just as Jaime was getting out of his pickup. "Hi," she said. "Thanks for coming to get me."

"I meant to be a gentleman and come to the door," Jaime said.

"Thank you, but I don't want my parents getting any ideas." Liza let Jaime open her door and slid into the cozy interior of his pickup.

When Jaime had buckled up and was exiting her driveway, he smiled. "If you're that worried about being seen with me, we probably shouldn't be eating in Echo Ridge."

Liza laughed. "I think we'll be just fine." *Breathe. It's only a business arrangement, Liza.*

"Well, you're the native. I'll follow your lead." Jaime headed out of the canyon, and Liza took a moment to collect herself.

"So, tell me a little bit about yourself." Liza leaned forward, admiring Jaime's handsome profile as he drove.

Jaime made a clicking noise and wrinkled his nose. "Since this is a fake engagement, can I make up stuff about myself?"

"No, because we already started the agreement with me telling you honest details about myself, so it's only fair that you reciprocate."

"Dang. Well, it was worth a try." He tapped the steering wheel. "Let's see. I have an interesting background. I was born in Costa Rica. My father is a Tico, and my mother is French. I speak French, English, Spanish, and some Chinese. Oh, and I like Nacho Cheese Doritos."

Liza laughed. "Okay, well, I can say that we have something very important in common, because Nacho Cheese is the only flavor of Doritos that should be allowed on shelves."

Jaime nodded. "Agreed."

"Seriously, though, I'm impressed," Liza said. "I can see why you run the business that you do—four languages!" She leaned back in her seat. "Have you been to Costa Rica lately?"

"Two years ago. I visited my parents there. It's a beautiful place. I thought about relocating there, but there are too many things in the States that I don't want to be that far away from."

Liza digested the information he'd shared, picking up on the rather cryptic details. "I've never been to Costa Rica, but it's on my bucket list."

Jaime smiled. "It's paradise. At least, I think so. There's so much to do between the ocean, the mountains, and the jungles."

"Well, I have to ask: if Costa Rica is so wonderful, what does keep you in the States?"

"Aw, she's perceptive. I could run my business from Costa Rica; that's for sure. But I got divorced last year, and it's been tough readjusting to the single life and trying to decide what I want to do with my life."

"So we both have scars on our hearts. Recent ones," Liza said.

Jaime parked the pickup in front of Jack's Pizza Shack and turned to her. "Yeah, I'm really glad most of the hurt is behind me. I hope you feel the same way."

Liza nodded. "I do for the most part. Once in a while I struggle, but I feel lucky, you know? I can't imagine my life if I would've married a lowlife like Mark."

"Unfortunately, I can imagine it pretty accurately,

because I did marry a lowlife. Now let's go eat some pizza."

He hopped out of the pickup, and Liza took that as a definite subject change. So maybe Jaime would be sparse on those details. It would take patience and a little encouragement to get him to open up. Liza was intrigued by the little that he had shared, and she wanted to know more.

Jack's pizza didn't disappoint. Liza and Jaime talked about the weather, work, and their parents until the pizza arrived. Then they focused on the oozing cheese hanging down the sides of each piece as they scooped it onto their plates. Liza popped a hot piece of pineapple in her mouth and closed her eyes. "The perfect combination of sweet and tangy barbecue sauce. Man, this is the best."

Jaime took a huge bite of pizza and mimicked her, closing his eyes and chewing. "Mmm."

They both started laughing.

Jaime wiped his mouth with a napkin. "I know you like pizza. What else do you like?"

"I like hiking. I like skiing up at Ruby Mountain, but it's hard to make time to get there." Liza considered whether she should share her secret goals. Jaime watched her attentively, and there was something about the look in his eyes that made her feel safe to talk to him. "I love writing. I'm working on a novel. I hope one day to be published."

"That's a perfect segue from a copywriter to novelist. I bet you'll get there." He nodded and took another giant bite of pizza.

Liza swallowed. He hadn't scoffed at her dream; he'd encouraged her and placed full faith in her that quickly. Liza's heart felt like the melted cheese oozing off the plate. *Business meeting!* "What about you? Are you living the dream?"

"Almost. There are some things that I want to do." Jaime looked down at his plate and cleared his throat. "Relationships I want to mend. And I want to expand my business."

Liza was just about to delve into that topic further, but she was interrupted by their teenage waiter. "You guys done yet? We're getting pretty busy in here, and we could use the table." He slapped a receipt down on the table.

Jaime turned his head, lifted an eyebrow, and motioned toward the pizza sitting in front of them. "We barely got our food five minutes ago. We'll need a little longer."

"How much longer?" The teenager flipped his shaggy red hair back as he spoke.

Jaime sat up straight. "This is a restaurant, and we are paying guests. It's bad form to hurry along your guests, especially when they haven't paid yet or included a tip."

The teenager's eyes widened. "Sorry, dude." He stalked off without another word.

Liza shook her head. "Wow, it's a good thing parents get their kids as babies first, because if they came as teenagers, no one would want kids. I can't believe how rude he was."

Jaime grimaced. "Yeah, teenagers are lacking in a lot of areas, but as long as he learns from the experience, he'll turn out okay."

"If you say so, but my hopes aren't that high." Liza picked up a piece of pizza and took another bite. Jaime seemed quiet, a little more pensive as he ate his second piece of pizza. She wondered if it was something she'd said.

Chapter Eight

Jaime finished off his third slice of pizza, still ruminating over Liza's comment about teenagers. He'd been trying to decide how to tell her about his son, but now he didn't think that would be a good idea. His fourteen-year-old son pretty much fit the bill she'd described for teenagers. Alex hated him, and Jaime couldn't do much to change his opinion, especially since he'd been the one to send him to boarding school. If only Alex could see that Jaime was trying to save him from Kori. His school counselor reported that Alex was a remarkable young man with a drive and focus that would bring him success. That was nearly opposite of what teachers had said when Alex lived with Kori.

"Either that pizza has blown your mind, or something has you occupied," Liza said.

He looked up and met her quizzical expression; there was a hint of a smile hiding behind her eyes. "How about both?" he asked.

"You can say that as long as you 'fess up to what has your wheels turning." Her full smile returned.

"I'm not sure I can 'fess up to anything that's going on in my mind right now. It might not be appropriate," Jaime hedged. He was rewarded with a blush creeping across Liza's cheeks. She looked down, and he reached his fingers out to brush over her hand. "I'm teasing, but I'd do it again to see you blush."

Liza laughed. "Stop it. And don't think I can't see what you're doing—changing the subject."

"Well, I was wondering if you remembered to get me a hotel room or if you're planning to share." He waggled his eyebrows.

"Yes, separate but adjoining rooms." Liza's blush turned a deep red, and she grabbed her water glass and took a drink.

Jaime chuckled. "Should we box up the rest of this pizza?"

Liza set her glass down and leaned forward, arching one eyebrow. "I think the question you should be asking is, who gets to take this pizza home?"

Jaime took out his debit card, grabbed the receipt, and waved it at the teenager. "We're ready."

The teenager hurried over and was surprisingly affable compared to their earlier interaction. He brought a box and helped clear the table. "Thanks for coming to Jack's. We'd love to have you come again."

Jaime nodded at the boy, his heart squeezing a bit at thoughts of Alex and what he might be doing tonight if they were still together.

Liza picked up the box of pizza and grinned. "Thanks for buying me dinner, but you don't think that just because you're a bachelor who paid for the pizza that I'm going to give up this box, do you?"

"You keep surprising me, Liza," Jaime replied. He stood and helped her out of the booth. When she set the box down to put on her coat, Jaime grabbed it. "And yes, I think the bachelor should always get the pizza."

Liza tilted her head and moved closer to him as they exited the restaurant. "Well, what about the bachelorette?"

Jaime snapped his fingers. "No fair. You play hard-ball." He held the box closer as he opened the door of the pickup for her. "How about you let me take this pizza home because I'm your fake fiancé?"

Liza climbed into his pickup and lowered her voice. "Who's faking?"

Jaime furrowed his brow and tried to think of a comeback.

She took advantage of his distraction and grabbed the pizza box. "Gotcha." She closed the door, her shoulders shaking with laughter.

He shook his head as he walked around the pickup,

and his own laughter bubbled up inside. Liza was fun, and it had been too long since he'd laughed. He climbed inside and was surprised to see the pizza box sitting on the console between them. "What's this?"

Liza shrugged. "You win. I'm taking pity on the bachelor, 'cause I bet you don't cook much."

"I cook all kinds of things," Jaime replied.

"Wait. Really? You cook?"

Jaime tilted his hand back and forth. "Enough that I don't have all the takeout places on speed dial."

"I figured." Liza let out a happy sigh. "Well, at least we have our story down for how we met."

"How's that?"

"The accident, silly. You pulled out in front of me, remember?"

Jaime made a point of keeping his eyes on the road as they drove up Main Street. "I remember that you ran into me."

Liza folded her arms. "I know the truth."

"So do I, and that's what is going to give me the most satisfaction—when I see the look on Mark's face."

"You know, I really think that despite the whole fake engagement thing going on, we're going to be good friends."

Jaime looked over and smiled at her. "Me too."

After he dropped Liza off and was headed home, he couldn't stop thinking about her friend comment. She had carefully placed him in the friend zone, but if it weren't for the fake fiancé bit, would he have had the guts to pursue her?

Chapter Nine

Liza worked late on Monday and Tuesday finishing projects and prepping for the conference. She thought of Jaime a few times, but besides sending him the conference details and her itinerary, she hadn't spoken with him since their pseudo date. As the time grew nearer to fly to Orlando, Liza doubted the validity of her plan. But every time she thought about chickening out and letting Jaime off the hook, she would remember Mark. He was tenacious and mentally unstable—not in a serial killer way, but he could probably be a serial killer's apprentice. Those thoughts kept Liza on track with her fake engagement plans.

Tuesday night, Liza worked on packing her bags and made notes of what else needed to be completed before her flight on Thursday. She had just finished polishing her brown leather boots when her phone chimed with an incoming text.

Liza picked up the phone and smiled when she saw Jaime's name on the screen.

Jaime: Hey, where did I propose? Or did you ask? ☺

Liza: Since I ran into you, I think it's only fair that you proposed. And hey, you really should send me your picture so I can add it to my contacts. You are my fiancé, you know.

Jaime: I can do one better. How about we take a selfie of us together?

Liza: Hmm, you're good. Have you done this before?

Jaime: LOL

Liza: So where did you propose?

Jaime: December 1ˢᵗ. Your front porch.

A thrill passed through Liza's middle. It was like a page out of a Christmas novel: her true love proposing on the first of December on her snow-covered front porch. She sighed and sent Jaime a very non-romantic thumbs-up emoji.

Liza wondered what would've happened if she hadn't asked Jaime to be her fake fiancé. Would he have asked her out on a date? She probably would never know the answer to that one, but a wistful part of her wished she could go back and undo the arrangement.

Her phone dinged, and she sucked in a breath when she saw a gorgeous photo of Jaime in their text messages.

Jaime: For now. Send me one of you.

Liza admired his light green eyes and the way his dark hair curled around his ear for a full minute before realizing that she needed to find a suitable picture of herself to send. She scrolled through her photos and found one that her sister had snapped last month when they'd visited the park near Chickadee Lake. The leaves had been perfect for raking into huge piles for her nephew to jump in and scatter everywhere. Lori had taken the photo of Liza grinning as Nate threw leaves in her hair. That was a happy day, and she'd had many happy days since. Liza sent the photo to Jaime.

He replied a moment later with one word. **Beautiful.**

Liza covered her mouth to hide her smile. Jaime thought she was beautiful. She shouldn't be smiling about it; he was her fake fiancé. She flopped back on her bed and looked up at the textured ceiling. She liked Jaime. There, she admitted it. If she liked him, then what better way to get to know him than by pretending to be engaged and spending time with him? It was a good thing no one else could witness her logic.

There was one thought that kept chipping away at her level of attraction to Jaime: she'd forgotten to ask him about the rumored DUI. Most likely, her subconscious had saved her from making a fool of herself. Jaime hadn't had anything to drink that night at Jack's Pizza Shack, but that didn't clear him. He didn't seem like the drinking type. Maybe she didn't need to worry about asking that tough question.

On Wednesday, Liza hurried into Stellar Ads and rounded the corner to edge into her cubicle before Rick noticed that she was ten minutes late. Nita was sitting in her office chair, moving slowly from side to side. Liza yelped. "You—you scared me to death!"

Nita smiled and leaned back in the chair. "Good. You deserve it for not giving me any details on your date."

Liza hesitated. She intentionally hadn't told Nita about her date with Jaime. "What date?" Better to play dumb.

"Oh no, you don't. Britta saw you go into Jack's Pizza Shack with a tall, dark, and handsome guy. Who is it?"

"Oh, that. It was just a business meeting. But he does live in Echo Ridge, so I convinced him to meet at Jack's." Liza kept her face neutral and prayed that the warmth she felt on her ears wouldn't spread to her cheeks.

Nita narrowed her eyes. "I think you're hiding something."

"And I think you're sitting in my chair, so get out or I won't tell you about how hot this guy is."

Nita clapped her hands and jumped up. "Oh goodie! I knew there was more. Spill."

"Well, it was a business meeting, and he's a really nice guy. I wouldn't mind going out with him again. I just don't know if it'll happen, so I don't want to get your hopes up."

Nita shook her head. "My hopes or your hopes? Because you should definitely get your hopes up, Liza. It's time for you to date someone. Do you have a picture?"

"Nita, do we have to do this now? You know Rick's going to be breathing down my neck any minute about the prep for this convention."

"All right. All right. But when you get back, we need to get together and chat."

Liza held out her pinky finger, and Nita curled her pinky finger around it. "Promise," they said together.

"Oh, and when you're in Florida, you have to go out for Cuban food. Take pictures so I can live vicariously through you."

"Cuban food? I don't know what to order," Liza protested.

"I'll take care of that," Nita responded. "Check your email by end of day, and all the deets will be there."

Liza laughed. "Okay, boss."

Nita nodded and exited the cubicle.

That had been a close one. Liza had stuck close to the truth, only leaving out a few details—the major detail being that Jaime was her fake fiancé. Or at least he would be her fake fiancé starting tomorrow and going through the weekend. She had been honest when she'd said she hoped for a chance to go out with him again. But she couldn't think about that right now. Too much work to do. Liza cleared all thoughts of Jaime's green eyes and strong physique from her mind and switched on her computer to pull up boring spreadsheets and notes for all of the contacts she hoped to make at the conference.

Chapter Ten

The flight to Orlando went by faster than Jaime could've imagined. Talking to Liza was easy, and when she fell asleep and rested her head on his shoulder, he leaned back in his seat ever so slightly and let his head lean against the top of hers. He couldn't remember the last time he'd felt so comfortable with a woman. Liza had found her way inside his heart in just a few days, and he was happy to spend time with her. That said, he was extremely nervous about his next move in their fake engagement.

The airline stewardess disturbed Liza's slumber with her noisy cart, and she awoke enough to receive a cranberry juice and some Biscoff cookies.

"I wish they had Doritos," Jaime murmured as he opened up his package of cookies.

"Right? We should lobby for that," Liza replied.

Jaime chuckled and sipped his Diet Coke. "I was thinking about your ring, and we don't want to give Mark any reason to believe this isn't real." Jaime tapped the simple gold band on Liza's ring finger.

"I know he'll ask to see the ring, but I hadn't thought about needing to impress him." Liza spread her fingers out and tilted her hand to the side, but the band didn't catch much light and it definitely didn't sparkle.

"Not necessarily impress him. More to cement the validity of this engagement." Jaime pulled out a small velvet bag from his pocket and passed it to Liza. "This was my mother's. I thought you could see if it fits."

"What? Really?"

Jaime nodded. "For the weekend."

Liza gasped when she pulled out the beautiful sapphire ring. The blue stone winked in the light, surrounded by diamonds. "But your mother is still alive. Why do you have this?"

"Her hands are too arthritic for rings anymore. She gave it to me on my last visit to Costa Rica. She told me to save it for someone special. I think she knew then that my marriage was failing."

"I'm sorry," Liza whispered.

"Don't be. I'm much happier now than I have been in years." Jaime was surprised by the sincerity of his own words.

Liza turned the ring around slowly, gazing at it from different angles. "Jaime, this is gorgeous. I—"

"Just try it on," he said softly.

Liza nodded, and Jaime watched as the sapphire ring slid neatly onto her finger. He felt an unexpected thrill when he saw the dark gem against her pale skin. When his mother had given it to him, he'd known it wasn't for Kori. Now, he saw that it fit perfectly on Liza. Everything about her easily fit into his life. This fake rapid romance was chipping away at the stone lining his heart. How could he tell Liza that he truly enjoyed her company without making things more complicated?

"Perfect," Jaime said.

"I promise I'll be so careful with it," Liza said. "It kind of makes me nervous to wear it, but thank you."

Jaime watched Liza tipping her left hand back and forth so that the light could catch the gem and make the diamonds sparkle. He rolled his shoulders back. Now wasn't the time to fall for Liza. He'd take this opportunity to get to know her, and maybe their friendship could develop after the fake engagement was over.

"I'm a ball of nerves." Liza held her hand over her stomach as they exited the airport. The conference center was only about twenty minutes away, and by the time they arrived at the hotel, Jaime had his own ball of nerves to deal with.

"What are we going to do the first time we see Mark?" he asked.

"Noodles." Liza's voice pitched up a notch with worry. "The farther we get into this, the more I realize I didn't think this through very well."

"Look, we're friends. I can honestly say that. I'm really glad we got to know each other, so let's just be friends."

Liza's shoulders relaxed. "You're right. I'm just over-thinking things. It's going to be okay."

"But did you just say something about noodles earlier?"

Liza laughed. "Oh that. Think of it as my pseudo-cuss word. I still live with my parents, you know."

Jaime laughed. "Got it." He loved the way that Liza's simple honesty and innocence made him feel at ease around her.

They pulled their luggage into the hotel lobby, and Liza's phone chimed just before they got in line to talk to the clerk. She pulled her phone out, glanced at it, and groaned. She flipped the phone toward Jaime. "Look."

Jaime furrowed his brow as he read the text.

Hey, babe-alicious! I'm at the hotel and I can't wait to see you!

"He still sends you texts like that?" Jaime asked in disgust.

Liza nodded. She threaded her arm through Jaime's, and they checked into the hotel. He didn't like how tense she was, and he hated to think that Mark had the power to unsettle her.

They had just started walking out of the lobby when Jaime saw the man who had his blood boiling. Mark was headed their direction, but he was busy scrolling through his phone.

There wasn't time to think. Jaime had to act now. "Liza, turn around."

She turned, her eyes widening as Jaime closed the gap between them. He swept her into an embrace and kissed her soundly on the lips. It was all supposed to be an act, but he felt the instant it changed. At first, Liza was stiff and surprised, and then she put her arms around his neck as she kissed him back. Every nerve ending in his body was suddenly charged and in tune with Liza. He pulled her closer and continued to kiss her, forgetting every concern he had from a moment before.

"Liza? Is that you?" Mark's nasal voice interrupted their kiss.

Liza moved to face Mark, but Jaime kept his arm around her waist so she could only turn partway. He leaned down and pecked her cheek as she answered Mark.

"Mark. I forgot you'd be here. This is my fiancé, Jaime Maldonado." She rose up on her tiptoes and kissed Jaime on the lips. She was smiling brightly, and Jaime detected laughter behind her eyes.

Mark choked on his words. He swiped a hand over

his light brown mustache, which was trimmed to perfection. He cleared his throat twice and tried again. "Your fiancé? You're engaged? You weren't even dating anyone."

Jaime stepped forward and arched his brow. "Liza and I are headed to our room. Have a good day." He gently tugged Liza's arm, and they walked past Mark as he sputtered to come up with a response.

"Liza, wait," Mark called.

"No, don't even look at him." Jaime held firmly to Liza's arm, and they walked directly into the elevator. Liza reached out and pushed the close door button three times in quick succession. The elevator doors closed just as Mark reached them, and Jaime caught a glimpse of the creep's angry red face.

Lisa put her face in her hands. "I thought he'd just leave me alone when he saw us together. What if this makes everything worse?"

Jaime put his arms around Liza and held her close. "I believed you, but I didn't understand how much he is affecting you. We're going to see this through, and you're going to be free of him once and for all."

"But you saw his face. He's mad." Her phone chimed, and she nervously swiped the screen.

"No." Jaime put his hand over her phone. "This has to stop. Block his number. There's no reason for him to contact you."

Liza bit her bottom lip, and Jaime thought he saw a

slight tremor there. He took a deep breath. How could he convince Liza that she was safe?

"I'm not going to let you out of my sight," he promised. "You're going to be okay." The elevator opened, and they walked down the hall toward their rooms.

Liza fished out the room key and waved it in front of the doorknob. "Will you come in with me and help me check out the adjoining doors?"

"Of course." Jaime held the door open as they both moved inside. He checked out the hotel room—a bed, a desk with a chair, and a tiny love seat took up most of the space. He unlocked the adjoining door on her side. "I'll go over to my room and be through in just a minute."

Jaime left his luggage in Liza's room and moved as quickly as he could out of her room and into his own. He didn't want to risk running into Mark in the hallway; it would be best if Mark didn't know where Liza's room was.

He unlocked the adjoining door and opened it slowly. "Hello?" He poked his head in and saw Liza sitting on the edge of her bed. Her cell phone was face down on the comforter, and she was staring out the window.

"I didn't read the texts, but I think he's sent at least five." She lifted her chin slightly. "Will you block his number for me?" She took a shuddering breath, and Jaime could see himself last year, coming out of the war zone with Kori. It had taken a lot of work in desensitization to quit reacting to Kori's manipulative games.

He sat next to Liza on the bed and picked up her phone. "Fingerprint?"

Liza held out her index finger, and Jaime pressed it on the pad of the phone to gain access. Sure enough, there were six texts from Mark, and Jaime clenched his jaw as he scanned the swear words and derogatory names that Mark had called Liza.

It only took him three seconds to delete the messages and block Mark. "There. You're safe."

Liza wiped her eye but didn't catch the tear trailing down her cheek. "I'm sorry. This is just so upsetting."

Jaime put his arm around her. "I'm sorry I kissed you. Mark was coming, and I didn't know what else to do. Was it that bad of a kiss?"

"No," she laughed, "it wasn't bad at all. Thank you. You really saved me back there. I don't know why I freeze whenever he's around."

Jaime had only been half kidding when he'd brought up the kiss. He couldn't resist smiling at Liza's response. He'd have to be careful, though. Sitting next to her left him wanting to hold her and kiss her all over again. He cleared his throat. "I used to do the same thing whenever my ex called me, but I'm okay now. She can say whatever she wants, and it doesn't bother me."

Liza looked at him and sniffed. "How?"

"Well, it wasn't easy," Jaime replied. "But I got to a

point where I realized I could stop the madness by deciding how I would respond."

"What do you mean?"

Jaime gently squeezed Liza's shoulder. "Mark can't hurt you anymore. I know it's easier said than done, but don't give him power over you or your emotions. If you get to the point where you can detach from all of the hurt and view him as the sick person he is, I think that's when you'll really find healing."

"I want to be there now."

"I get it. But in this moment, you need to recognize your emotions, own them, and then let them go."

Liza looked down at her hands and wiggled her left finger. The ring winked back up at them as it caught the light. "Okay. I can do that."

"Good, because we're in Florida and we should definitely do something fun before the conference gets underway tomorrow." Jaime pressed a kiss to her forehead and assured himself that his wildly beating heart was in anticipation of a few days off in a warmer climate. Yeah, it was just Florida, because he couldn't let it be Liza.

Chapter Eleven

Liza took a twenty-minute nap and retouched her makeup when she awoke. She changed into the light-yellow sundress she'd packed and couldn't help but smile. December fourth in Echo Ridge, New York, would never allow her to work in a sundress. She intended to soak up the sun, take in extra vitamin D, and lift her spirits regardless of the situation before her. She still had a nervous tremor when she thought of Mark in the same building, but then she focused on Jaime. He had been so kind and understanding. She closed her eyes and relived the moment when he'd put his arm around her and kissed her forehead. They were friends, but maybe if she could stop freaking out over Mark, there might be a chance for more.

Jaime knocked four times on the adjoining door. His

eyebrows shot up when Liza opened it, and he said, "Well, you look amazing."

Liza ducked her head and smiled. "Do I look like I belong in Florida?"

"No, you look like you belong right here beside me. I'm going to enjoy this fake engagement. Let's go."

Liza giggled. She took Jaime's hand as they walked out into the hallway. They took a stroll around the hotel grounds, admiring the palm trees and flowering bushes. Liza especially liked the bougainvillea with dark pink blossoms trailing along the deep green foliage. It was eighty degrees out, and the sun warmed her skin as she walked beside Jaime.

"Feeling better?" Jaime asked.

Liza nodded. "I was thinking we're in this mess because I slid on icy roads, but I can't complain about the sunshine. How about you?"

"I agree. I'm actually really looking forward to the conference. It was nice of you to give me ideas of who to approach."

"You're very talented," Liza said. "I've been doing my homework, and I'm really impressed with your company."

Jaime's cheeks darkened with what looked like a bit of a blush. She loved that he was so down-to-earth. She'd done a little more checking on Jaime and he had an extremely successful business, but he wasn't arrogant about it. His company had grown enough that he had multiple employees and a waiting list for some of the services they offered.

"You should know that there are a lot of people that try to do what you do, and they fail miserably. You should be proud of yourself."

"Oh, I don't know. I have a lot of limitations, but I do enjoy my work."

Liza rolled her eyes. "All anyone has to do is a little bit of shopping online to recognize how important language skills and translation are in advertising. Give yourself some credit. You're not only helping the consumer to have a better experience; you're truly impacting the businesses you work with."

Jaime's left dimple creased again. It gave Liza a little thrill, because it only showed up when he smiled big. "Thanks, Liza. That means a lot coming from you."

"It's only to butter you up so you'll walk the extra six blocks to get Cuban food with me."

The dimple stayed put. "Well, I can't say I disagree with your methods. I'm hungry."

"Me too."

"Is Cuban food your favorite?"

"I've never tried it. I'm a chicken alfredo with broccoli kind of girl."

"That sounds good too. We could do that if the Cuban food doesn't pan out." Jaime quickened his step to catch the next streetlight before the walk signal turned off.

The walk ended up being almost eight blocks, but the weather was perfect and the Cuban restaurant was authentic and delicious.

"How'd you find this place?" Jaime asked around a mouthful of mojo chicken and rice. "I think I can taste the orange juice they used on this chicken. Delicious."

"I didn't. My friend did, and she insisted that I take pictures and send them to her. You ready for a restaurant selfie?"

"Sure." Jaime slid closer to her in the booth and held up a forkful of maduros, which they had discovered were deliciously sweet fried plantains.

Liza snapped the picture and then took a few individual photos of the plates of food. A close-up of her beef-stuffed empanadas would surely send Nita into a food frenzy. Liza sent them off to Nita, who replied in about one nanosecond.

Who is the model, and where can I have some of him and what he's eating?!

Liza barely restrained a laugh. She was thankful she hadn't shown Nita a picture of Jaime when she'd asked before. Now she could be vague and not have to be interrogated about it.

Liza: Just having dinner with some of the people from the conference.

Nita: Well, box him up and bring him home!

Liza sent a smiley face and sipped her Sprite. When

Nita found out that Jaime was Liza's neighbor, Liza would never hear the end of it.

By the time they finished their meal, Liza realized she hadn't thought about Mark since she'd left the hotel. She wanted to keep it that way. "Jaime, thanks so much for doing this. But I still feel like you know more about me than I know about you."

"Oh no. Don't start the interrogation process again, please?"

"You know, you're almost good-looking enough to get away with that." Liza winked. "Almost. Now spill: what brought you to Echo Ridge?"

Jaime held her hand as they walked back toward the hotel. "Well, I needed a change of scenery, and I wanted to get far enough away from Kori—that's my ex-wife—so that she couldn't just drop by my place."

"Did she do that often?"

"Let's just say that I have learned something about emotionally unstable people." He took a deep breath. "They don't know how to manage their own emotions, so the only way they can exist is by eliciting emotional reactions from others. When you try to starve an emotional bottom-feeder like that, you get people like Mark and my ex-wife. It's not normal. It can't be explained. And to most people their actions seem harmless."

Liza felt a weight lift off her chest. Jaime understood her at a level that almost no one else did. "I've had so many people tell me what a nice guy Mark is and that they can't believe he dumped me the way he did. No one has seen what went on before and after the breakup."

"Exactly." Jaime released her hand and pushed his fingers through his hair. "It about made me crazy at first. The kind of behavior that Kori exhibited isn't healthy, and people don't want to hear about that kind of stuff. They only want to hear about the sordid details, like how they cheated on you."

"What happened in your marriage? What made everything come tumbling down?" Liza appreciated how Jaime guided her across the street, his hand at the small of her back.

Jaime pressed his lips together and hesitated before answering. "I had to get off her emotional roller coaster. It was dangerous, and it was ruining my business. I'm not sure of all the things she was involved in and frankly, I don't want to know. I just feel lucky that I got out alive."

Liza thought about Jaime's words and how they coincided with the thoughts that she'd had recently concerning Mark. "It's kind of weird to think of something as major as a broken engagement and your divorce as a good thing, but I learned it can be."

"Yep. My parents have been asking the same questions you have, though. They can't understand why I'd want to move to the mouth of a snowy canyon in Echo Ridge when I could go stay with them in Costa Rica."

"Well, I can't fault their logic there." Liza brushed the hair away from her face. "But until you live in Echo

Ridge, you don't really understand how wonderful it can be. Our community is magical, tight-knit, with so many good people. I love our little library. I love the bed-and-breakfast—it's called the Emerald Inn. I love the events out at the Big Barn Boutique and how everyone goes to the lacrosse games at the high school. And even though the winter is a little colder than I'd like most of the time, I love each of the four seasons."

"I like it too. The winter is colder than my parents will ever dream of in Costa Rica, but that's okay, because when I was married it was winter year-round."

Liza hesitated and then laughed when she caught his meaning. "Hey, I was thinking about what you told me about your ex. Do you have her number blocked?"

Jaime grimaced. "As much as I'd like to I can't just block her and write her out of my life. There are some issues, but I can set boundaries and keep my shields up so she can't get the response she's looking for."

"I'm glad that you've shared this side with me. It gives me hope that I can do better."

Jaime put his arm around her and gave her a squeeze. "You're going to be awesome. You've just taken some important steps. Getting married is a bonus too." He winked and tapped the beautiful sapphire ring on her finger.

Liza batted his hand away. "You are a tease, you know."

"Who's teasing?"

Liza sucked in a breath. For a second, Jaime really did look serious. Was he saying that he truly had feelings for her? Then he grinned and tugged on one of her curls. Liza giggled, grateful she hadn't explored that thought too long. "Just so long as Mark doesn't hear any different."

By the time they returned to their rooms, Liza was exhausted, and she still had to review a few things before the conference started. She and Jaime said good night, and Liza closed their adjoining door before preparing for bed. It was comforting knowing that Jaime was just on the other side of the wall. He'd given her great advice and wonderful support that day. She hadn't realized just how much Mark was affecting her until Jaime suggested blocking him from her phone. Why hadn't she severed that tie six months ago when he'd first started bothering her about getting back together again? She could admit now that she had been worried about the fallout. But those worries were over. She'd set things in motion today to give herself real emotional freedom.

She was also seriously enjoying every moment she spent with Jaime. The weekend hadn't even started, and already she was worried about it ending. Would they see each other back in Echo Ridge, or would it be business as usual? It was better not to worry about that right now, but Liza couldn't help it—she liked Jaime. A lot. She washed her face and then sat on the edge of the bed. What had she been thinking?

She wasn't thinking, because she'd never imagined that she could fall for Jaime—or that she'd have a chance with someone like him. They had a great connection that couldn't be faked. The only problem was that the pretending could get in the way of their opportunity to see if they really liked each other. *Calm down, Liza.* Florida was a long way from New York, and she'd take off the beautiful engagement ring long before they reached Echo Ridge.

Liza reviewed all of the logic behind her decisions, but she couldn't control everything. If something were to go wrong with their fake engagement and word got out, she'd die of embarrassment. To be the girl who got dumped twice. That wasn't a reputation she could write herself out of.

Chapter Twelve

Friday morning, Liza received a text from her boss at seven o'clock.

Rick: Mark says he can't reach you. Wanted to make sure you're still planning on your meeting with him at 11 today?

She growled and punched in a reply: **Yep, I'll be there. I have the schedule.**

Rick responded with a thumbs-up. Liza briefly thought about sending him a different finger emoji, but she put her phone away instead. She needed this job, and she still wanted to apply for the promotion. A lot was riding on her performance at this conference.

Liza applied her makeup and pulled on dress pants and a dark pink blouse. She curled her hair and pinned it up on one side. The light brown curls looked good against the pink. She wanted to look beautiful and businesslike. Jaime would tell her if she'd hit the mark.

She knocked on the adjoining door and waited with a bright smile on her face. When Jaime opened the door, she lifted one arm. "What do you think?"

"You're going to kill it today," Jaime said.

"It or him?" Liza asked innocently.

That garnered a deep chuckle and the appearance of Jaime's dimple. "What about me?" he asked, motioning at his shirt. It was dark blue with light blue dots on the perfectly pressed material. Her eye was drawn to the collar and cuffs, which were lined with a contrasting light blue fabric. He wore black dress slacks and polished black dress shoes that Liza guessed were Allen Edmonds.

"You look great. Very professional and handsome."

Jaime stepped into her room. "Thank you, but if I'm standing next to you, no one will know I'm there. You're gorgeous, Liza."

Liza felt heat flood her cheeks. "Thank you."

"You ready to do this?"

"Yes. Let's grab breakfast, avoid Mark, and woo some new clients."

"Sounds like a plan," Jaime replied. His phone started buzzing, and he pulled it from his pocket. Glancing at the screen, he said, "I'm going to step in my room and take this. I'll be quick." He shut the door behind him as he said hello in a friendly voice.

Liza's smile faded, and she was reminded again just

how little she knew about Jaime. What if he had a girl-friend? He'd never mentioned dating anyone, but Liza hadn't specifically asked either. Fake engagements were a lot of trouble, but so were real ones—at least in her case. Liza shrugged and packed her shoulder bag, double-checking that she had enough business cards and flyers for all of her potential contacts.

Jaime was only gone ten minutes, and when he returned, they went down to breakfast. He didn't mention his call, but Liza could tell that something was on his mind. He drowned his waffles in butter pecan syrup.

"So, I'm guessing you take sugar in your coffee?"

Jaime chuckled. "Correct." He speared a bite of waffle with syrup dripping in a steady stream and shoved it in his mouth. "Mmm."

Liza took a bite of her ham-and-cheese omelet and tilted her head. "Mmm. Mmm."

"What? You think your breakfast is better than mine?" Jaime said before taking another bite of soggy waffles.

"Slightly less prediabetic, but it looks like you're enjoying that, so I won't judge."

"Ha, you were judging me before I even took a bite." He swirled another bite in his pond of syrup and waggled his eyebrows. "But I understand. You're not used to living on the edge."

Liza tilted her head. "On the edge of what?"

"Life." Jaime popped in another bite. "Today I want you to try to relax and find enjoyment despite the conference. And tonight, let's do something fun."

"Like what? I'm supposed to be working until six o'clock." Liza held out a foot clad in beautiful dark pink heels with gold accents. "Do you really think I'll be able to walk by then?"

"You have other shoes, and I know they aren't snow boots, so we're leaving this place at six. You'd better start thinking."

"Where's this bossy side coming from?" Liza cut another piece of omelet and struggled to keep a straight face.

Jaime's eyes were sparkling as he answered. "I'm your fiancé. I'm allowed to boss you around if it means you get to enjoy being in Florida."

"Okay, then, I'm up for the challenge."

"That's good. I promise your feet will be glad."

Liza's middle tingled with fireflies not drenched in butter pecan syrup. She enjoyed bantering with Jaime— or flirting, if she was being daring. But she couldn't lose her head. Jaime was just playing his part. She needed to play hers. "So, just to review. We'll try to keep each other in sight, and if I need your help, I'll blow you a kiss."

"I like it. And if I need your help, I'll just find you and kiss you."

Liza laughed and ducked her head so Jaime wouldn't see the blush creeping across her cheeks. "All right. I'm going to go start making the rounds, and I'll see you about ten thirty so we can prep for the appointment with Mark."

"You got it. You're going to do great, Liza." Jaime stood and brushed off his pants. "Hey, I'm so glad you had this idea, because it got me to come to the conference. This is just what I needed to get some new blood flowing in my business and move to the next level."

Liza stood and put her hand on his arm. "Thank you." They walked toward the conference center together, and Liza steeled herself for the inevitable meeting with Mark. She only hoped that he wouldn't run into her before their appointment that day.

Chapter Thirteen

Jaime was a hot mess, and it had nothing to do with the weather in Orlando. Sure, the balmy eighty degrees warmed his skin and made him long for Costa Rica, but only if he could take Liza with him. And therein lay his problem. He was deceiving Liza every day—not lying to her face, but omitting the truth, because she still didn't know that he had a son. Jaime loved Alex and he'd do anything for his kid, which was why he'd kept him a secret from everyone in Echo Ridge. Part of it stemmed from his own shame. Jaime wished he could go back and undo the damage that Kori had inflicted on their son, but he couldn't. However, he could prevent future damage to his son by protecting him. If that meant keeping him a secret, Jaime was willing to do that. It still didn't feel right to deceive Liza, but he was afraid of what Liza would think. Especially after her comments on teenagers at Jack's Pizza. And especially because now she would think he'd agreed to be her fake fiancé for his own benefit.

Earlier, he'd taken a call from his friend Jared, and it seemed like great news on the surface. Jared was an attorney and had reviewed Jaime's case for gaining more custody of Alex. He told Jaime that if he was in a stable relationship it would help. "Don't go out and get engaged, but just think about the future. The judge won't want to take Alex from his mother to go live with a bachelor."

The words kept repeating in Jaime's mind. *Don't go out and get engaged.* What would Jared think if he knew what Jaime was doing right now? For a moment, Jaime had considered telling Jared he was dating someone, but he didn't. The fake engagement was to protect Liza and help her keep her job.

But was it really so bad if he benefited too? Even as he asked himself the question, the answer slapped him in the face. He needed to be honest with Liza, but he didn't know how and his own insecurities made it that much more difficult. What would she do when she found out that he had a son who hated him? Jaime rationalized that it was okay to wait because she had so much going on dealing with Mark and her boss. That Rick dude definitely deserved his nickname; Jaime had heard Liza muttering it under her breath when Rick had texted her more details about the meeting with Mark as they'd walked into the convention center.

There were easily two hundred booths in the giant room, and nearly every single company could be a potential client. He'd meant it when he'd thanked Liza. Her scheme might have been a little crazy, but he was determined to grow his business while he protected her.

Jaime had scouted out the locations of prime targets for his business. He was also confident of where Mark's booth was situated in the huge room. As Liza turned left to meet one of the companies on her list, Jaime made a beeline for Mark's booth. His steps slowed as he approached, and he scanned for Mark. He swallowed when he saw Mark bent over a stack of papers. Mark's light brown hair was perfectly styled with honey-blond highlights that made Jaime cringe; any guy who spent more time and money on his hair than his female counterpart was suspect. His minimalist mustache didn't help either.

Jaime waited until Mark looked up, almost as if he sensed Jaime staring at him. Jaime strode right toward Mark's booth and made eye contact with the slimy creep who had caused Liza so much grief. When their eyes met, Jaime narrowed his and lifted his chin a fraction of an inch. With his head held high and posture erect, he passed by Mark's booth. He counted five steps, turned slightly, and looked at Mark again. Mark's eyes widened as if he was surprised to be caught staring at Jaime. Jaime nodded once and turned on his heel, continuing past the booths in that area.

There, the threat had been delivered. Mark knew Jaime was here, and unless he was a complete idiot, he knew that if he messed with Liza, he'd have Jaime to deal with.

It only took a minute for Jaime to locate Liza in her bright pink blouse, talking to another businesswoman at a graphic design company. He smiled as he walked past, and when Liza smiled back, his heart thumped hard in his chest. In that moment, he realized he wanted Liza to be happy and he'd do anything to protect her. If it meant smashing in Mark's face in the public arena, so be it. The only problem was, how could he be sure of Liza's feelings for him? They were friends and they were acting like a couple in public, but what would happen when they were on the plane ride home?

Chapter Fourteen

A t ten thirty, Liza slipped into the ladies' restroom and re-applied her lipstick. She took three deep breaths and looked at herself in the mirror. *You can do this*, she thought. With a smile, she exited the restroom and saw Jaime leaning against the wall.

He pushed off and walked toward her. "Hey, beautiful. You ready?"

A thousand butterflies took flight in Liza's stomach. Jaime was irresistible, the way he filled out a dress shirt and those dress pants. But it wasn't just his clothes. His presence was calming yet invigorating, and Liza found herself craving his touch. "I'm almost ready. We have a few minutes, and I want to introduce you to a guy named Parker. I think he is a star candidate for your company."

"You're amazing."

"Why?"

Jaime put his hand on the small of her back and gently pulled her closer. "Because you're working a job, keeping a radar out for your crazy ex, and you still have the mental capacity to find leads for my business."

Liza smiled. She put her hand on Jaime's arm and squeezed. The silky smooth material of his dress shirt allowed her to feel his toned bicep. "Well, don't thank me yet. Let's go talk to this guy."

Jaime leaned in and brushed a kiss across her cheek. "I'm thanking you now."

Liza turned and they walked back into the conference area. It was then that she saw Mark heading their direction. Jaime deftly steered them away from him, and Liza took up the lead to direct him to Parker's booth. After the introductions, Liza had a moment to consider whether Jaime had kissed her cheek because he had seen Mark approaching or because he really wanted to. Maybe Jaime was wondering the same thing about her being on the receiving end of his kiss.

Focus, Liza. It wouldn't do her any good to be distracted when they went to the meeting with Mark. Ten minutes later, Jaime had information and an appointment with Parker. They walked toward Mark's booth, and Liza linked arms with Jaime.

"I owe you, Liza. That was an excellent lead. I can't wait to get started." He took her hand and interlaced his fingers with hers.

"And that's only one lead. Just think how many you'll have by tomorrow at day's end."

"With you on my side, I'll be golden." He squeezed her hand, and Liza felt the butterflies take flight again. Jaime stopped her about ten paces before Mark's booth. "I'm going to kiss you because he's watching."

"Okay." Liza didn't have time to say anything else or prepare herself, because Jaime's lips were covering hers. Even though the kiss only lasted about five seconds, the warmth of his lips lingered after they parted. Forget the butterflies. She had hummingbirds bumping up against her rib cage, fireworks shooting from her heart, and lips that wanted to be kissed again. Jaime took her hand again, and they walked toward Mark's booth and sat down in the chairs. Liza imagined what it would be like to be kissed by Jaime every day.

"I'll be right with you," Mark said as he hovered over his computer, trying to appear as if he hadn't been gawking at them.

Jaime looked at Liza and she could see the question in his eyes. Almost as if he was asking her if she was all right. She put her right hand up to her lips and blew him a soft kiss. Jaime grinned and chuckled, tightening his grip on her fingers.

Mark sat down at the table in front of them and placed his hands beside a stack of papers. "I'm so glad you could make time in your schedule for me Liza. I feel privileged to be talking to one of the up-and-coming editors at Stellar Ads. Looks like all that time you spent writing is paying off with Rick."

Liza didn't allow herself to be baited by his bland praise. Mark knew about her dreams of becoming a writer, and he'd made a lot of disparaging comments to her while they were engaged. She pretended that he was just another agent who wasn't right for her work. She wouldn't let his rejection sting.

"What projects would you like to discuss?" Liza asked. She dipped into her shoulder bag and pulled out a piece of paper, which she handed over to Mark. "Here you'll see a listing of some of our most popular services. We'd be happy to create a tailored package for you."

"Would that involve one-on-one consultation?" Mark asked in a sultry voice.

Jaime leaned forward. "Yeah, I hear Rick does a lot of consultations. Liza can get you set up with him."

Mark flinched, but he wasn't swayed. "Liza, dear, Rick indicated that you'd be willing to work with me on this big project. I don't want to sign off to somebody that's too busy to give it the attention it needs."

Liza choked back on her horror as she realized that Mark was willing to create an advertising project for the sole purpose of torturing her. Rick would force her to work with him, because for all intents and purposes, Mark's requests would seem legitimate. She felt Jaime's hand on her leg, pressing gently. She remembered what he had said about Kori. Mark only had power over her if she gave it to him.

Liza took a breath and looked directly at Mark's beady little eyes. "I'd be happy to help you. However, I don't do one-on-one consultation. Rick does, but he generally charges double the fee of our package prices." Liza tapped the paper so Mark could note the price.

His eyebrows rose slightly. He straightened and pointed at her hand. "You have a beautiful engagement ring. I can see that your fiancé has good taste." Mark looked at Liza's ring finger and then flipped his gaze toward hers.

"Thank you," she said with as much venom in the phrase as she could allow.

"So when's the wedding?" Mark leaned forward. "You know I love weddings. I hope you'll send me an invitation."

It was all Liza could do not to gag, but she forced herself to look in his eyes. "This is a business meeting, Mark. If you don't have any further questions, I will wait for you to contact Rick. I hope you enjoy the conference, and if you can't find any new clients on your own, I'm sure that you could meet someone to steal them from."

Liza pushed back her chair and stood up, spinning easily on her three-inch heels.

"I'm not finished with this meeting. I still have other considerations I'd like to discuss." Mark stood as well, splaying his hands on the table and leaning forward.

Jaime stood and put his hand on Liza's back. "Liza's answered all the questions you need, and luckily for you, she's very thorough in her prep work. The paper she gave you outlines all the details you'll need. Good luck."

Mark was still sputtering as they walked away.

Liza's head ached, and she had an uneasy feeling settling on her shoulder blades. "He's probably going to call my boss and complain."

Jaime frowned. "If your boss can't see what Mark's trying to do, then he's an idiot."

"Obviously he can't see it, because he forced me to meet with Mark in the first place," Liza replied. "Where are we going?"

"Back to the hotel for a few minutes. I need a breather, and I bet you do too."

Liza thought about protesting. There were still so many people she was supposed to talk to, but Jaime was right. She needed to clear out Mark's bad vibes and reset her system in order to continue for the rest of the day. "I have a headache coming on."

"I'm sorry. But I know just the thing to fix that." When they reached the hotel lobby, Jaime nudged her into the little food mart. He grabbed a package of choco-late-covered raisins and a bottle of Diet Coke. "I'll grab some ice, and that headache will be history."

Liza looked askance at the junk food and rolled her eyes. "At this point, I know better than to argue with you."

"What were you saying earlier? That you didn't know enough about me?"

Liza rolled her eyes again, and Jaime barely held back a laugh.

A few minutes later, they were situated in her hotel room with an ice-cold glass of Diet Coke and a pile of chocolate raisins. Liza had kicked off her heels and sprawled across the bed as soon as the door had closed.

Jaime lounged on the little sofa, looking out the window. "You know what else might do you good?"

"No, but I'm sure you'll tell me."

"A little more sunshine. We should walk around the hotel grounds, soak up some vitamin D, and then get back to work."

"Right after I take a fifteen-minute power nap," Liza replied.

"That sounds like an excellent idea." Jaime hopped up from the sofa and headed through the adjoining doors. Liza could see him fiddling with his phone, probably to set a timer on his way out.

She smiled and rolled over, closing her eyes. She cleared her mind with two deep breaths in and pushed thoughts of Mark away with two breaths out.

True to his word, Jaime returned fifteen minutes later, and they spent five minutes walking in the sunshine before returning to the convention center. They were both so busy for the rest of the day that Liza hardly had time to think about Mark and his slime factor. Just before six, Liza had met all of her goals for the two-day conference and felt relieved that she would be able to exceed Rick's expectations. All except where Mark was concerned.

Jaime was talking to another prospective client when Liza's phone buzzed with an incoming text.

Rick: I got an interesting message from Mark today. Said the meeting didn't go as well as he had hoped and wondered if there was a chance you could meet with him again Saturday? Did he talk to you about this?

Liza looked up and saw Jaime handing a business card to a man and woman in another booth. He was calm, cool, and collected. He didn't let anything ruffle his feathers. How would he respond? Liza pursed her lips and decided to take charge of her life.

Liza: Yes. Actually, we covered everything in the meeting, and I left him with extra information. From this point on, he wants to work with you directly. If he says differently, it's probably just because he's trying not to hurt my feelings. Thanks for the opportunities. This convention is going well!

Liza held her breath as she waited for Rick to respond. When she received a thumbs-up, she wanted to cheer. She couldn't wait to tell Jaime. She had carefully disentangled herself from Mark without making waves at work. At least, that's what she hoped.

Chapter Fifteen

❧

The convention center was emptying quickly as the clock ticked past six. Liza wondered if she looked as tired as her feet felt. She and Jaime had walked around booths for the last hour, meeting people and collecting business cards. A woman approached them, and Liza remembered meeting her earlier. Her name was Margo, and she worked with a company that designed banners for elementary schools.

"A bunch of us are headed to the bar down by the pool. Want to come along?" Margo asked.

"I just need to change out of these heels and take a breather first," Liza responded.

She looked at Jaime, and he nodded, although he didn't look enthusiastic about the idea.

"We'll see you two lovebirds later," Margo said.

As soon as she was out of earshot, Jaime said, "I'd rather not go to the bar. It's just not my scene."

"Me neither, but it is a good way to network." As soon as Liza had finished her sentence, she remembered the rumor about Jaime and his drinking. She still hadn't asked him about the DUI. They stepped inside the elevator, and she leaned against the wall. "Jaime, do you have a drinking problem?"

Jaime's shoulders fell, and a sigh escaped in the quiet of the elevator. "I used to. It was a short phase. I'm not proud of it, but it's how I coped for a while after my divorce."

"I'm sorry. I didn't know. We definitely don't need to go to the bar."

Jaime rubbed his hand over his forehead, closing his eyes. "There's more you should probably know. I'm surprised you haven't heard already."

Liza waited. She didn't want to attempt to fill in the blank with what she'd heard.

"When I first moved to Echo Ridge, I was arrested for driving while intoxicated."

"Oh." Liza waited two beats before asking, "So you decided to stop drinking after that?"

Jaime lifted one shoulder and let it drop. "That's what I told myself, but occasionally I still had a drink." The elevator opened, and they walked down the hall in silence. Liza opened the door to her room and motioned for Jaime to come inside. He followed somewhat tentatively. "I'll understand if you're angry about this. I probably should've told you sooner."

Liza folded her arms and looked at him. "If you still have a problem with it, then yes, you should have told me, but if it's under control, it's in the past."

Jaime sighed again and sat down in the chair. He kicked his shoes off. "I wanted it to be much further in the past. But that morning I pulled out in front of you, I'd had a lot of trouble sleeping and ended up taking a drink. I haven't had a drink since."

"Were you drunk that morning?" Liza couldn't keep the judgment from her voice.

"No. No. It just scared me 'cause I realized how much trouble I could be in if I'd been in an accident and drank enough for another DUI."

"Still, that's beyond irresponsible."

"I know. You're right. That's why I decided right then to stop." Jaime looked up at her. "That's why I won't go to the bar tonight even if it means missing out on networking."

Liza felt hurt, even as she told herself that it was illogical. She didn't know Jaime—couldn't expect to know everything about him in a week. But then the realization hit her like a bucket of cold water. "That's why you didn't want to call the cops. That's why you agreed to everything—because you were afraid of getting another DUI."

The look on Jaime's face could be placed next to the

definition of chagrined in the dictionary. "I'm not proud of it," he murmured. "I made a lot of mistakes."

"I wish you would've told me."

"There really hasn't been many openings to say, 'Hey, I have a DUI on my record.'"

The hurt multiplied, and Liza's lungs felt tight. The room was too quiet. "I feel really stupid. I thought you were doing me a huge favor, when all along I was playing right into your hands."

"That's not fair. We made an agreement, and I'm keeping my end of the bargain."

"Is that all this is, then? An agreement?" Liza's voice rose, and it wobbled a bit on the ending.

Jaime pressed his lips together. "I don't know, Liza. We're pretending. This is all fake. I don't know what the rules are."

His words felt like a slap in the face. She looked at him and then down at the floor, nodding slowly. "You're right. We are pretending. This was my idea. I thought we were friends, though, and I'm generally honest with my friends." She thought about Nita and the truth she'd kept back about Jaime. That was different, wasn't it?

"I wasn't lying to you. I'm honest with my friends too."

"Just because you didn't tell me a lie doesn't mean you're not lying to me. If you misled me, let me believe things that aren't true, that is the same as lying to me."

Liza meant every word that she said. She wasn't angry. She was disappointed.

"You're right. You deserve better than that. Look, I want to be honest—"

"Me too. And if I'm being honest, then right now I need a break. I'll talk to you tomorrow."

Jaime stood with a confused look on his face. "But I thought we were going out."

"No. I'm tired and my feet hurt. Thanks for your help today." Liza stood and followed Jaime over to the adjoining door. She waited for him to go through, and then she shut hers and locked it. Part of her wanted to be dramatic and slam it, but life wasn't a drama.

Do not cry, Liza told herself. She got herself into this mess, and she could be a big girl and see it through. If only she could understand why she felt so hurt that Jaime was keeping secrets. Why did she feel like she had a right to his secrets? And why did it hurt so much when Jaime had reminded her that they were just pretending?

Her cheeks burned with embarrassment. She hadn't been just pretending today. When Jaime nuzzled her neck and kissed her cheek, it had sent a thrill through her like nothing she'd ever experienced before. Liza put her face in her hands and groaned. She'd made a mess of things and overreacted when she should've been understanding of Jaime's situation. But she didn't know how to fix it now.

She took a hot shower and then wrapped up in a

towel and lay down on the bed. The headache had lurked in the background for most of the day, just waiting for its chance to return. Maybe she could nap for a few minutes and things would make sense when she awoke. She fell asleep faster than she would've guessed.

The next thing to enter her consciousness was a loud noise. Liza squinted at the digital clock on the night-stand. It was eight thirty; she'd been asleep for an hour. She rolled onto her back, trying to pinpoint what the sound was. Had it been a knock on her door? She held still and listened, but there were no other noises.

Stretching her arms overhead, she got up and slipped on her pajamas. Hunger was gnawing at her stomach. That noise still bothered her, so she tiptoed over to the main door and looked through the peephole. No one stood outside her door, but she could see the edge of what looked like a tray. She opened her door a crack, and she was rewarded with the sight of a room service tray and a delicious aroma that set her stomach to roaring.

A card on the tray had her room number written on it. She picked it up and flipped it over, gasping when she saw a smiley face next to Jaime's name. Lifting the tray carefully, she went back inside her room, setting it on the bed. When she took off the silver cover, her mouth watered. "Chicken alfredo. He remembered."

Suddenly she felt like crying again, but Liza wrote it off as hunger and fatigue mixed with too many emotions.

She scooped up a bite of the noodles dripping with white sauce and devoured it. It was absolutely delicious.

Jaime had only left a smiley face on the card, but the noodles might as well have spelled out his apology. And for how good they tasted, Liza accepted it. Now it was time for her to bridge the gap. She felt awkward, almost like she'd been sucked back to her teenage years. Jaime was kind and thoughtful. He'd stood up for her and went well beyond the role of the fake fiancé.

Once she'd eaten, Liza walked to the balcony, opened the sliding glass door and stepped outside. Maybe some fresh air would give her an idea of how to remedy her current situation.

"Nice out here, isn't it?"

Liza jumped and covered her mouth to stifle a scream.

Jaime was leaning over his balcony. "Sorry, I didn't mean to scare you." He looked somber. No smiles.

"I'm just a little jumpy." Liza leaned forward. "Thank you for dinner. It was delicious and such a nice thing to do."

Jaime shrugged. "Figured if you were half as hungry as I was, it wouldn't go to waste."

"But you remembered. It's my favorite." Liza rested her cheek in her palm and looked at Jaime. "I'm really sorry that I overreacted. You have a right to your secrets. You have your own life, and I have mine. I'm sorry I crossed the line. Can we still be friends?"

"Of course." Jaime stood up straighter. "They are my secrets, but I want to share them with you. I guess it was hard to know how much I could trust you, but once I did know, then I was sort of a coward."

Liza gripped the railing and leaned forward. "I'm a coward. I haven't been standing up for myself and my life. I've been letting people cross every boundary and break every rule. You taught me in just a few days what I need to do to make a change. I won't forget that."

"Well, I don't want to be a coward anymore. I want to tell you —"

Liza's phone started ringing. She hesitated and looked down. "It's my mom. Do you mind if I take this?"

Jaime nodded, his smile faltering. "Go ahead. I should probably call my mom too."

Her mom was calling to tell Liza that Sharla had passed away earlier that afternoon.

"Oh, Mom, I'm so sorry. I'm glad you're there to help Marianne. Does she have other family coming?"

"Yes, but I've been with her most of the day. We were hoping she could last until Christmas, but Sharla insisted that she was going to celebrate Christmas in heaven."

Liza smiled. "It sounds like she was at peace."

"Yes, she was," Mom replied. "And I know the pain was intense the past week. She's finally at rest."

"I'll add Marianne and her family to my prayers. I would have loved to have you with me here in Florida, but I'm glad you stayed home."

"Me too. You take care of yourself, and don't work too hard."

"Okay. Love you, Mom."

By the time Liza got off the phone with her mom it was getting late, and with the early start in the morning, she figured it was best to leave things as they were with Jaime. It seemed like he'd been about to tell her something, but she didn't want to press him. Instead, she sent a text thanking him for dinner again and wishing him a good night.

Jaime texted back a minute later: **Sweet dreams. I'll see you in the morning.**

Liza smiled and hugged her phone. They hadn't exactly sorted everything out, but she felt better about her fake fiancé. Good enough to face another day.

Chapter Sixteen

He'd been so close to telling her about Alex. But once the moment had passed, Jaime didn't know how to recapture it. They didn't see much of each other during Saturday either; they worked nonstop, separately circling in the large conference area as they spoke with different business owners and took down potential client details.

Maybe he'd find an opening that night. They were planning to walk down to get a hamburger and fries for dinner. He'd found a diner that had been featured on one of the many foodie shows he'd watched, and he'd convinced Liza to go for standard American fare. He hoped that the diner would live up to its hype. He also hoped that something in the food would induce his honesty. If he couldn't find a way to tell Liza tonight, then he'd take her out on a date when they got back and tell her then. The pressure of the fake engagement would be off, and they could start over. Jaime looked in the mirror and straightened the collar of his dress shirt. Confident with his new plan, he walked over and knocked on the adjoining door.

Liza answered, and his breath caught in his throat when he met her eyes. Her face was bright and just a tiny bit sun-kissed from their walks in the Florida heat. When she smiled, her brown eyes danced, and it took all of his concentration not to stare at her full pink lips. Maybe they'd be in luck later and run into Mark so he could kiss her again. He only felt a little guilty for that thought.

"You look beautiful, Liza, and happy too."

"I am happy. We made it through this conference, and we get to go home tomorrow. No more pretending."

"Yeah, and all kinds of great business potential in the works." Jaime's spirits fell a notch. He didn't want to stop being with her, but he didn't want to pretend either. He had developed feelings for her, and he didn't know how to convey the truth of those feelings in their current fake engagement.

"I'm starving. You said the diner is close by?" Liza grabbed her purse and slung it over her shoulder.

"We'll be there in five minutes if we walk fast and hit the lights right." Jaime held out his hand, and Liza took it as they exited the room.

They rounded the hallway to the right and saw Mark

a split second before he saw them. "I need to talk to Liza," he said.

"No, you don't," Jaime replied tersely. "The conference is over."

"Liza, please," Mark implored, and somehow, he made his eyes appear shiny with unshed tears. "I still love you. Why won't you give me a chance to show you how much I care about you?"

Liza straightened. "I want you to leave me alone, and if you care about me, you will stop harassing me."

Mark stepped forward, but Jaime moved in front of Liza. "She didn't stutter."

"You think you can just take her away?" Mark spat.

"I'm not taking her away, because she wasn't yours. Just because you realize now that you made the worst mistake of your life doesn't mean that you can change things." Jaime stepped forward, looking down at Mark. "Don't talk to Liza again. You're not a part of her life, and you never will be."

Mark glared at Jaime. "This isn't over." He gasped and dodged to the side when Jaime lifted his fist. "I'll call security!"

"Go right ahead." Jaime continued to lift his fist upward until he rested his chin on it and looked at Liza. Her lips twitched with a barely concealed smile.

Mark huffed and stomped off. To her credit, Liza was stoic and she held her ground, not even flinching as Mark stalked past her.

Jaime pushed the elevator button and ushered Liza in through the doors as they slid open. He turned and pulled her into a hug. "Are you okay?"

"Yes, thank you."

Jaime held her and didn't say anything until they'd exited the elevator. He took her hand again. "I don't want him to ruin our night."

"I'm worried that Mark will say something to my boss about me being engaged."

"He shouldn't say something about that. It's totally unrelated to business," Jaime replied.

"I know, but Mark is weird like that. He likes to gossip. Why didn't I think of this possibility?" Liza pushed her palm into her forehead.

"Why didn't you think of every crazy scenario your ex is capable of? Because you're not crazy, and I'm glad." Jaime gently removed her palm from her face.

"But what if he says something?"

"We'll roll with it." Jaime lifted his shoulders and let them drop. "Let's keep in touch, and if you need to play this out a couple more days, it's all right." Jaime felt the edge of a lie on the tip of his tongue. He still hadn't told Liza about Alex. There was no way he could tell her now, not if he wanted her to speak to him again. She might not forgive him as it was because he should have told her right at first. He thought back to what Alex had said about Jaime replacing Kori. If only there was a way to prepare his son for a future that would never include his parents being together. He hadn't told Liza, but it was time to face the hard things and be truthful. Once they returned to Echo Ridge and the fake engagement was over, he'd tell her everything.

Chapter Seventeen

Liza was a goner. After witnessing the scene with Jaime and Mark—which could have come straight out of the most romantic film—her heart would never be the same. Jaime had spoken with such conviction when he'd told Mark that it was the worst mistake of his life to let Liza go. Her chest warmed with the sentiment he expressed. She would write everything in her journal app tonight with the full intent of including it in her next novel. Hallmark would love a scene like that—the kind that made the audience cry and hearts swoon.

During dinner, they talked about the success of the conference while outlining ideas for some of the different clients they'd met.

"You know, you have a lot of business sense that goes beyond copy editing. I think Rick is missing out by not giving you more opportunities."

"Thank you." Liza popped a fry in her mouth. "That's part of the reason I had to make this conference work. Rick has been talking about promoting me."

"Just don't let him dangle that carrot too long," Jaime said after swallowing a mouthful of burger. "You're worth more than that, and if Rick can't see it, that's his loss."

Liza pointed a French fry at him. "You say that as if there are tons of jobs available in Echo Ridge."

Jaime snatched the fry from her fingers and popped it into his mouth. "Maybe it's time you looked outside of your hometown?"

Liza huffed and picked up another fry. "It's complicated. I pay rent, which supplements my parents' income. I don't want to leave them in the lurch."

"That is complicated." Jaime dipped a bite of his burger in the barbecue sauce. "If you're serious about it, though, talk to your parents. Give them a heads-up and propose a timeline. Tell them you're planning to move in six months, and that gives them a chance to prepare for the reduction to their income."

Liza nodded. "That's a good idea. I really love Echo Ridge. I wish there were more job opportunities." She didn't really like this conversation. She loved Echo Ridge, and she liked Jaime too. Maybe he didn't like her as much as she thought; otherwise, why would he be talking to her about leaving the town when he was staying put? Her excitement over his chivalrous actions earlier faded a bit, but she wouldn't let that stop her from enjoying the steak fries and the specialty barbecue sauce.

They finished dinner and walked casually back to the hotel. "Thanks again for bringing me along, Liza," Jaime said. "I had a great time."

"Thanks for agreeing to my crazy scheme. Only one more day and you'll be free again."

He put his arm around her as they approached the doorway. "It's been kind of nice. I hope you won't be a stranger."

Liza wiggled her ring finger in front of his face. "I think I'll miss this. You can't believe the compliments I've received for 'my ring.'"

Jaime chuckled. "I'm glad it could be appreciated, even if it was only for a weekend."

"Good night, Jaime. I'll see you in the morning."

Liza went into her room and started packing her things for the early flight. She'd learned some things about herself this weekend. Jaime was right: it was time for her to make some changes. Either she needed to get the promotion at work, or she would have to look for a new job, even if that meant moving away from Echo Ridge.

Jaime ended up sleeping most of the flight home, and Liza finished writing in her journal app about all the details of the weekend. She smiled to herself when she thought of how she could use the events of her and Jaime's fake engagement for a romance novel. For fun, she brainstormed a few ideas and even wrote a scene where the fake fiancé professed his love for the darling girl that he never would've met if he hadn't pulled out in front of her on an icy road.

After that, she scrolled through her Kindle app and selected a few new books to read over the holidays by Jeanette Lewis, Cami Checketts, and Cindy Roland Anderson. If she were a millionaire, she'd tell Rick, "Yes, please," the next time he threatened to fire her, and she'd stay home and read books for the rest of the winter. Unfortunately, she wasn't a millionaire, but maybe if she could learn to write like some of her favorite authors, she could change her fate.

When the plane landed, Liza checked her emails and texts. There was a particularly annoying email from Chrissy demanding that Liza get her report in before Monday. Liza frowned and deleted the email.

"What's the matter?" Jaime asked.

"Oh, it's just work. There's this girl at the firm, and she is the epitome of rich, snobby troublemaker. She's one of those kids who was sent away to boarding school, and she acts like she owns the world." Liza took a deep breath. "I honestly hate working with her."

"So boarding school made her that way, or she just is

that way?" Jaime leaned forward, studying Liza's face as if her answer really mattered to him.

She sighed. "I don't know. Why have kids at all if you're just going to send them away and make someone else raise them?"

"So they can get an education that they couldn't get at home?"

"Wait, did you go to boarding school?"

Jaime chuckled. "No, I just have a different perspective on it."

"Well, none of my children are going there. If there's even a miniscule chance that boarding school influenced Chrissy, I don't want to take my chances."

They deplaned and hurried out of the airport, shivering at the frigid temperatures that were at least fifty degrees colder than Florida. Jaime's pickup was covered in snow and New York was definitely showing off its winter skills. They cleared off the snow and ice and turned the heat up on the drive home. Jaime seemed distracted as he drove, almost like he wanted to talk to Liza about something but couldn't bring himself to do it. He started and stopped his sentences a few times before settling on the weather and how Christmas was right around the corner.

"If you haven't made it to Kenworth's department store, make sure you get there," Liza supplied during another awkward pause.

"Is there some shopping I need to do?" Jaime asked innocently.

Liza pushed his shoulder. "Yes, you'd better take advantage of the shopping countdown, but that's not why you should go to Kenworth's. They have a hope tree every year, and the community helps provide information for individuals in need. They hang little ornaments on the tree that have gift requests." Liza smiled and leaned back in her seat. "I just love going there and seeing all the ornaments disappear. It's fun to choose someone and buy a gift for them without knowing who they are or what their circumstances might be. I like thinking about the families who are touched by the special Christmas spirit."

Jaime looked at her, and she noticed that his eyes seemed to be a lighter shade of green. He was studying her so intensely that she forgot what she'd been saying.

"What?" she asked.

"I love your heart," he said quietly. "I love how you see and experience the world. I'm hoping a little of that has rubbed off on me. I'll definitely go over to Kenworth's. Is the tree easy to find?"

Liza's heart beat stronger with his words, and she felt herself falling a little more in love with him. "I love your strong heart. You have courage and wisdom that I hope has rubbed off on me. And yes, the tree is easy to find. Right in the clothing department, usually by the women's section."

"Liza, I wanted to tell you ..." Jaime looked over at her and then focused again on the snow-banked roads.

Liza waited, but he didn't finish his sentence. "What did you want to tell me?"

Jaime swallowed and reached his hand out to cover hers. "I wanted to tell you thank you for not judging me because of my past. I want to do better and be a better man."

"I could say the same thing to you, except for the better man part. I want to be a better woman."

Jaime squeezed her hand, and Liza tried to calm the galloping horses racing through her chest. They were alone. The engagement was over, and Jaime was saying nice things to her and holding her hand. Did she dare hope that this moment was real?

Before she could contemplate the divide between reality and fantasy, Jaime had pulled up to his house, where Liza's car was tucked secretly away in his garage. They made a quick transfer of bags, and Liza backed her car out and waved at Jaime. There was no parting hug or kiss, and Liza felt the absence of his affection. She wondered again if she would ever really know if Jaime had feelings for her.

It must've snowed six more inches while they had been in sunny Florida. Liza pulled into the driveway, got out, and stamped her feet to keep the snow from going down her low-heeled boots. She had her left hand on the doorknob to walk into the house when she saw a glimmer of light and gasped. She was still wearing Jaime's mother's ring! There was no time to think, because her parents had certainly heard the garage door open. She stuffed the ring into her jeans pocket and walked inside.

Her mother was heading her direction and pulled her into a hug. "It's so good to see you. And look, Reuben—she's stolen some sunshine."

"Yep, sun-kissed. You look good, Liza," Dad said.

If only her parents knew just how kissed she'd been over the weekend. "I can't believe how much it snowed while I was gone. Sorry I couldn't bring some sunshine home with me."

"I like the snow," her dad replied. "No weeds to pull."

Mom chuckled and patted his cheek. "Plenty of things to fix in this old house, though."

That comment reminded Liza of the conversation she'd had with Jaime. Along with paying off bills, her parents were using the rent money to repair all sorts of things around the house as well as create a buffer for future expenses. The pattern they'd created was comfortable, and she hated the thought of disrupting it now.

"I'm going to go unpack and jot down a few more notes before tomorrow." Liza escaped to her room and quickly texted Jaime.

I am so sorry! I still have your mother's ring. I can drop it by your house.

Jaime: Go ahead and drop it off on your way

home from work tomorrow. I know you have a busy day ahead of you.

Liza: Okay, I promise to keep it safe!

Jaime: I know you will. I trust you.

Liza kept looking at that word in his text. Trust. He said that he trusted her, but did she trust him? That quality was key to a successful relationship—even a friendship. Hopefully tomorrow she'd have a chance to chat with Jaime about how to go from fake fiancés who kissed and held hands to just friends. She brushed her fingers over her lips, almost wishing she'd never tasted Jaime's kiss.

Chapter Eighteen

Even though Liza was exhausted the next morning, she arrived at work right on time. She was hoping to have a few moments to put together her thoughts for her meeting with Rick. She slipped into her cubicle after checking to see if Nita had arrived. That was funny; Nita was never late. Liza sent her a quick text asking if she was feeling okay.

Nita: Just running an errand for Rick.

Liza: This early? My goodness! See you soon.

Liza finished typing up her notes and printed off a full sheet of contacts and leads that she had gathered at the conference. If Rick was anything but pleased, she might have to seriously consider Jaime's advice to get a new job.

"Surprise!" Nita called out. The office was suddenly a flurry of balloons, flowers, and Christmas cupcakes.

Liza tried to take it all in as Elaine pulled her from her chair and hugged her. Over the shoulder of her coworker, Liza read the words printed on the Mylar balloons.

Congratulations!

You're engaged!

Happy ever after!

Her stomach dropped to her toes. She couldn't swallow fast enough, and her eyes were burning.

Nita approached her with the biggest smile on her face. "I don't know how you could do it, but you are pretty good at keeping secrets."

What could she say? Liza scrambled for words. "Um, how did you find out? I haven't told anybody yet."

"Well, taking your fiancé to the conference is a pretty big tell, wouldn't you say?" Rick's voice boomed from behind her. Liza jumped as Rick patted her on the back. "Congratulations!"

Liza cleared her throat. "Thanks."

"Let me see your ring."

The ring. She would just have to tell them. This was all a huge mistake. Her face was burning, and if she didn't get a hold of herself, she was going to start crying. She had to think fast.

Jaime's ring was in her car. "Oh my goodness. The ring. I'll be right back!"

Liza jogged out of the building before anybody could

say another word. She scooted into her car and opened the glove compartment. She had placed the ring in a small padded envelope last night. She dialed Jaime's number while pulling the ring out.

Jaime answered on the second ring. "Liza, how are you?"

"Jaime, I'm in a mess! My office is throwing a party for me because they found out I got engaged!"

There was a beat of silence. "What?"

"Everyone in my office thinks I'm engaged! Mark must have told Rick because he knew that you came to the conference with me."

"Oh no."

"Rick sent Nita to get balloons and treats and flowers and everything. This is a disaster!" Liza blinked rapidly to keep the tears from falling.

"Wait, it doesn't have to be a disaster. We can fix this." Jaime's voice was low and calm. "Let me think. There must be something we can do."

Liza looked down at the ring in her hand and took a deep breath. She tried to think, but her mind was under attack from a volcano of emotions and a mountain of regret.

"Liza, what do you want to do? If you want to play this out for a little while longer, I'll support you in that. If you want to go in there and tell them they made a mistake, I'm okay with that too."

"Oh, Jaime, I don't know what to do. Mark will have a

heyday with this when he finds out I have another broken engagement. This is why they teach you in church never to lie. Why did I think I could get out of a lie any different than anyone else?"

Jaime chuckled. "Now don't take yourself straight to Hell yet. You're a good person, and you have a lot to deal with. Your plan was a good one, because you were able to get through the conference pretty much unscathed and send a message to Mark that you were unavailable."

"I wish I had thought of another bright idea." She hadn't anticipated Mark's scheme to work with Stellar Ads. If she admitted that she wasn't engaged, he might pursue her with more tenacity.

"Well, I don't wish that," Jaime replied. "Put that ring on your finger and go back in the office. Stop by my house after work, and we'll talk."

"But are you sure? This will ruin any prospects you have of dating. You know Echo Ridge is a small town. I'll have to leave work at lunch to tell my parents!"

"Liza, remember where my reputation was before I met you. I wasn't dating much and I didn't have many friends, but now I have you. If you'd like me to go with you to see your parents at lunch, I'll do that."

Liza sucked in another breath and tried to see out her window. She'd fogged it up pretty good with all of her frantic talking. She looked at the ring, slid it on her left hand, and straightened up in her seat. "Okay, we're engaged. I'll be at your house at noon."

Liza got out of the car and walked back into her office, ready to celebrate her fake engagement as if it was the most authentic thing that had happened to her since she'd been engaged over a year ago. There was a way to fix this. She didn't know what that way was yet, but hopefully Jaime would have some ideas.

Chapter Nineteen

When Jaime hung up the phone, he stared out the window for a full minute, trying to digest what he had just agreed to. The fake engagement was never supposed to leave Florida, but now he'd given Liza permission to bring it to the close-knit community of Echo Ridge, New York.

His phone rang, and Jaime glanced at the caller ID. It was Jared, his acting attorney and friend.

"Hey, Jaime, have you thought anymore about what I suggested?"

"You mean how I'm supposed to write to the judge claiming that I have a stable home?"

"Yeah, that. I want you to get that sent over to me."

Jaime hesitated as a thought struck him. "How might it change things if I were engaged?"

"What?" Jared laughed. "You serious? You got engaged? I didn't even know you were dating!"

Jaime's mind whirled with the possibilities he was diving into. This was the point of no return, and he didn't want to listen to the good angel on his shoulder telling him, "No!" Jaime took a breath and replied, "Well, I kept things quiet, and I sort of wanted it to be that way because Kori is so crazy. So I hope you don't mind if we hold off on lots of details for now."

"Well, you'd at least better give me her name."

Jaime took a deep breath. Was he really going to do this? "Liza Sorensen. She lives here in Echo Ridge. She is absolutely beautiful, smart, and she makes me happy."

"Dude, I can hear it in your voice. You haven't sounded this good for a long time. Congratulations."

"Thanks." Did he sound happy? It was hard to tell with the trepidation and guilt crawling down his spine.

"Hey, you might spill the beans a little and see how Kori reacts. She might go just crazy enough to give the evidence the judge needs."

"I don't know about that," Jaime said. "I think she'd try to manipulate Alex more than she already does to get revenge."

"Well, she's obviously going to find out. Record everything and screenshot your texts. I want a mountain of evidence."

"Will do." Jaime ended the call and contemplated the rapid turn of events.

His head was spinning. This fake engagement was never supposed to benefit him, and now Jared had shown him a way that it actually could. He would never know if it was good or bad timing; Kori texted him a few minutes later.

Kori: I'm going to make sure you never see Alex again. You are the worst father! You were never there for him, and you're never going to change!

Jaime stared at the phone, letting his anger simmer just below the surface. Kori had abandoned him and Alex when their little boy was only four years old. She'd come back three weeks later claiming that she was renewed, changed, and would be a better mother. Jaime never knew all the details of what happened when she'd left, but it broke something in his heart that day. He'd held on for another nine years—much longer than he should have. Kori had probably been stealing Alex's pills from the very beginning. Jaime had hoped that the divorce would end the bitter abuse from Kori and free Alex from their constant warfare, but it seemed like Kori would never give up.

And he had fallen in love with Liza—a woman who didn't even know he had a son. When Liza had started ranting about boarding school, the chance to tell her blindsided him and he'd been a coward. He didn't want Liza to think his son was a problem. Even as his conscience pricked him with the knowledge that Liza would be understanding once she knew more about the situation, Jaime hadn't given her the chance. Was he more afraid for Alex or himself?

He definitely was afraid of what Kori would do when she found out he was engaged. She would likely pull Alex into the middle and turn him against Liza before she even had a chance. For now, he'd keep things quiet and hope that the news of his engagement didn't go beyond Echo Ridge.

Chapter Twenty

The Christmas cupcakes were made with red velvet cake mix and cream cheese frosting. The white frosting was sprinkled with red and green balls and a light dusting of silver powder. Almost too pretty to eat, but since Liza was nearing a meltdown, she had two of them before lunch. When coworkers asked, she stuck as close to the truth as she dared in relating her and Jaime's whirlwind romance. She texted Jaime to let him know that they had met in November, so they'd at least known each other one month before he'd proposed.

"I know you're holding out on me," Nita said. "But I'm a patient woman, and I *will* get every last detail on this guy."

A nervous tremor moved through Liza's stomach. She believed Nita. It was imperative that she see Jaime and talk through the details before anyone questioned him.

For now, Liza turned to Nita and pulled up the picture of Jaime and her at the Cuban restaurant. "He's a wonderful guy."

"Yummy!" Nita exclaimed as she bit into a creamy cupcake. "And I'm not talking about dessert." Then she paused. "Wait a minute. I recognize him. He's Florida!"

"Actually, he's Echo Ridge, but he went to the conference with me," Liza said. "He ran interference for me and kept Mark off my back. We had a wonderful time."

"What? Liza! You did not tell me your fiancé went with you to Florida." Nita put her hand on her hip and tapped her foot.

"He owns a business that translates and edits for websites, so the conference was a great place for him to pick up leads," Liza explained.

Nita shook her head. "I can't believe how much I've missed. You are going to catch me up, but first I have to send in a report. Let's do lunch soon."

"Yes, I'm excited for you to meet Jaime." Liza infused as much excitement into her voice as she could muster, but it still fell a little flat to her ears. Had Jaime considered what it would be like to meet family and friends while pretending to be her fiancé? It was never supposed to go this far, but they were in it neck-deep now. Liza sighed and tried to focus on her work.

Liza left her office amidst more congratulations at noon. By the time she reached Jaime's house, she'd almost talked herself out of the whole charade. She hurried up the steps and the front door swung open before she could knock.

"Liza, come in." There was no hint of stress in his eyes. How could he be so calm?

"I don't know if we should do this." Liza wrung her hands. "I think I should go back to work and say, 'April Fool's!'"

"But it's December eighth." Jaime helped her out of her coat and motioned for her to come into the kitchen. "I made us some lunch."

"You didn't have to do—mmm." Liza smelled the aroma of chicken noodle soup. She saw a stockpot on the stove. "You made soup?"

"Yes. Comfort food." He proceeded to dish up two bowls. "So how are we going to tell your parents?"

Liza groaned. "I don't know. They'll think I'm crazy."

"A valid point." Jaime slid a bowl in front of her and pulled out a box of club crackers.

"Rick told me that he wants to talk about my meeting with Mark when I get back from lunch. I don't know what's going on, but I refuse to work with him." Liza took a bite of soup. "This is delicious. Thank you for feeding me."

"I'm glad you like it." Jaime took a few bites and then

said, "Don't you think being engaged is still a good defense against Mark?"

"See, that's the thing. This guy I know taught me something important over the weekend. I realized I need to stand up for myself and draw clear lines. I don't need to hide behind an engagement to do that anymore."

Jaime's spoon clanked against his bowl. "Are you saying you want to call off the engagement?"

Liza sniffed. "I'm saying I don't think it's worth the cost."

"But Liza, we're already in it this far, and it's working. Why not play it out a few more weeks? We don't have to set any dates or have anything concrete."

Strange that Jaime seemed more keen on the engagement idea than she was. "We could, but then I want to tell my parents the truth. It's not fair to them to think that this was all real when it's a lie."

Jaime thought about that as he swallowed another bite of soup. "I like that idea. We don't have to worry about my parents, because they aren't on social media. Luckily, Costa Rica is far enough away that even the busiest busybody of Echo Ridge won't reach them."

Liza laughed. "One problem solved."

"Hey, I know. What if we tell your parents that we really hit it off and we were just talking about getting engaged when someone overheard?"

"And then my work heard about it and threw me a party and we went with it?" Liza picked up a cracker and dipped it in her soup. "That would make so much more sense."

Jaime patted her on the back. "See, we'll get through this somehow."

"I still don't know, but I'm willing to try it." Liza finished up her soup. "Although if you hadn't fed me this soup, I think things might be very different right now."

"Ah, food is a weapon in my arsenal," Jaime mused.

Liza patted his cheek. "Don't worry. I'll figure out your weakness soon enough."

"I thought it was you." Jaime winked at her, and Liza's heart danced the Charleston. If Jaime didn't stop flirting with her, she might have to kiss him for good measure. Jaime cleared the dishes and Liza watched him work for a minute, oddly comforted by his routine motions.

She stood and moved in front of the large picture window in his living room, staring at the beautiful winter scene. The evergreen trees stood so peaceful, yet powerful with their branches drooping under the heavy snow. The forest seemed to extend forever beyond Jaime's yard. Part of Liza wanted to run into that forest and hide from the mess she was in. The other part wanted to curl up in Jaime's arms and fall in love for real.

Chapter Twenty-One

J aime's idea turned out to be a huge success, because he had Liza's parents laughing over the fumbled proposal. He assured them that his intentions were pure and that he would take good care of their daughter. "We got engaged unconventionally, so I told Liza if she ever has second thoughts to toss me out on my ear. We're taking things slow, even though it appears that we've jumped the gun."

"The way he uses clichés, though, makes me worried for what he's going to say in our marriage vows," Liza retorted.

They left her home in very good spirits, and Liza received a text from her mom gushing over Jaime.

He is very handsome, funny, and kind. I'm nervous but excited for you at the same time!

"So my mom approves of you, but she's a little nervous," Liza said.

"Understandably," Jaime replied. "So how long are we going to keep this up?"

"The engagement? At least until Christmas is over, right?" Even as she said the words, she hated to think of not seeing Jaime every day.

"Or maybe even New Year's?"

"I think you're starting to like me a little bit." Liza nudged Jaime's elbow.

"Oh, I like you a lot." Jaime lifted his eyebrows and winked. "And there's always kissing to ring in the New Year."

Liza laughed and turned her face toward the window so he wouldn't see the heat she felt in her cheeks.

Jaime chuckled. "But seriously, we won't have to go to any parties by ourselves, right?"

"That is a definite perk to being engaged," Liza replied, feeling her face cool just a bit. "Although Rick is so cheap, his Christmas party is held a few days before Christmas during lunch, and it's for employees only."

"I would make a comment about him being cheap, but then how would I look since I'm not throwing a Christmas party for my company?"

"That's different and you know it."

"Yeah, kind of hard to do when the company is online, but I should probably at least send them an ecard with their Christmas bonus." Jaime pulled into his driveway and cut the engine.

"It's cool that you even do bonuses."

"And even cooler that your parents totally bought our story."

"Don't you feel just a little bit guilty about it, though?" Liza rubbed her arms and shivered at the escaping heat.

"I do, but I'm trying not to stress over it, because I know that we'll make it all right in the end."

Liza nodded. "I certainly hope so." She still had to go back to work where she would accept congratulations from excited coworkers. It would be difficult to get any real work done, but maybe if she adopted Jaime's mindset —that everything would be all right in the end—she could make it through the day.

On Tuesday, Liza finally made it through her report with Rick. She carefully sidestepped any mention of Mark, and when Rick brought him up, she deftly changed the subject. She wouldn't be able to hold Mark off forever if he was determined to work with Stellar Ads, but she was ready to put her foot down if it came to that.

"You keep up the good work and that promotion is as good as yours," Rick said.

"Thanks." Liza had been hearing that line for at least

three months, and she was starting to doubt Rick's sincerity. She turned in her application to make everything official, hoping that it might move things along. After the meeting, she felt drained and more than a little discouraged. Her work wasn't fulfilling. Sure, she'd honed her writing skills, but she wasn't getting anywhere.

Every night, she worked on her novel and researched publishing. One route was the traditional course with an agent and a publisher. Another route was to be an indie author and act as her own representative. She would be responsible for every stage of her book's production. It seemed overwhelming, but she liked the idea of having more freedom, especially after working for a man like Rick. Maybe Jaime would have some good insight on her writing career.

Jaime. Every time she thought of him, she felt a little thrill followed quickly by a hint of doubt. He always seemed authentic when they were together, but she kept reminding herself that even their friendship had been built from false motives. Liza sighed and rested her head on her desk.

"I know the feeling," Nita muttered.

Liza jumped and swiveled in her office chair. "I told you to quit sneaking up on me."

"You're invited to my ugly Christmas sweater party." Nita handed Liza a glossy postcard invitation featuring a family in ugly sweaters.

Liza laughed and snorted at the same time. "Nita, you kill me."

"It's this Saturday. Prize for the ugliest sweater." Nita tapped the postcard. "Bring your hot fiancé too."

"Oh, believe me. I will." Liza only felt a little guilty at how excited she was to have yet another reason to spend time with Jaime.

Chapter Twenty-Two

Racing thoughts about the relationship he needed to mend with his son kept Jaime awake most of Thursday night. Sometimes in his weak moments, he wanted to give up and just let Kori win, but then he would think of the times he'd spent with Alex. His son was a great kid who had been handed a raw deal by his parents. Jaime decided to call his son and test the waters regarding his relationship with Liza.

It was Friday afternoon before Jaime worked up the nerve to call Alex. He waited until he was sure that school was out, said a prayer, and pushed call.

"Hey, Dad," Alex answered in a chipper voice.

"Hi Alex. You sound happy that it's Friday."

"I am because it's almost time for Christmas break."

"Great. I'd love to have you come visit me. There is a great ski resort only fifteen minutes from my house."

"I don't know. I'll have to check with Mom."

Jaime didn't point out that the divorce decree outlined the days Alex was supposed to stay with him. He didn't want to force the issue. If Alex wanted to come and visit, he'd be ready. If not, he'd try his best to stay involved in his son's life. "I wanted to talk to you about something you said last time we were on the phone."

"Oh, what?"

"You mentioned something about me replacing your mom and I wanted to let you know that your mom will always be your mom, but she and I are both dating other people."

"You're dating someone?" Alex's voice pitched higher. "Why?"

"Because that is what single adults do. They date so that they can make new friends and maybe even get married again." The conversation would have been better in person, but Jaime had no way of knowing when he'd see his son next.

There was a beat of silence before Alex asked, "Dad, are you going to get married again?"

Jaime swallowed. "If I find the right person, then yes, I want to get married. And when that time comes I hope you can be friends with her."

"Friends with a stepmom? Everyone knows that step-moms are evil."

Jaime chuckled. "I'll do my best to find one that isn't."

"So you and Mom really aren't going to get back together?" Alex sounded younger than his fourteen years when he asked the question.

"No, Son. I'm sorry for how the divorce has affected your life. I hope one day to spend time with you so that you can understand why I had to make the choices I did. I'm happy now."

"Mom doesn't want you to get remarried. She said that then you'll ignore me."

Jaime gritted his teeth. It wasn't a surprise that Kori had said such inappropriate things to their son, but he wished there was a mute button for her rants. "I'm here for you. It's hard when you never come to visit, but I do want to be part of your life. Do you understand that?"

"Yeah, but I hope you don't have a girlfriend yet. It would just be too weird."

"Well, the woman I'm dating is special to me. I'd like you to meet her sometime."

"I don't want to do that, Dad. I gotta go, okay?"

Jaime's heart pinched at the change in his son's tone. "Okay, have a great weekend. I love you."

Alex hung up without saying goodbye and Jaime held his phone tightly as he tried to figure out how to navigate the situation before him. He didn't like the feeling that he needed to choose between Alex and Liza. After so many years of unhappiness, why couldn't he love his son and pursue a relationship with Liza?

Jaime rolled his shoulders back and switched gears to

finish up his work for the day. It was much easier to problem-solve work issues than to think about his messy relationships. He took a moment then to jot down a few ideas before his next meeting with a contact he'd made at the All-Star Design Conference. Meeting Liza had brought new life into his business, but it also had him looking at his personal life in a different way. Jaime worked hard until five and then hurried to get ready for a date with Liza. He chose a dark green button-up shirt paired with jeans and a black wool zip-up sweater. Liza had mentioned that they needed to go shopping for their ugly sweater party, and Jaime wanted to be sure to dress opposite that role for this evening.

Since everyone knew about their engagement, Jaime could walk up to the front door to greet Liza and her parents. When he saw Liza, his breath caught in his throat. She was a vision in a stunning turquoise sweater that angled above her knees. She wore the sweater over black leggings that accentuated her nice calves.

"You look beautiful." Jaime leaned forward and brushed a light kiss on her lips. When he pulled back, Liza's cheeks were pink.

"Thank you," she said breathily. "You look mighty handsome yourself."

"Okay, lovebirds," Reuben interrupted. "Be careful, and watch for black ice."

"I will. Have a nice night, Adina. Keep Reuben out of trouble." Jaime winked and helped Liza out to his pickup.

"My parents really like you," Liza said. Jaime thought he detected a wistful tone in her words.

"The feeling is mutual." He recognized that this could be an opener for more heavy subjects, so he deftly changed gears. "Ugly sweaters and then Kenworth's?"

"I know we need to drop into the thrift store, but then can we walk down the street and look at the window displays?" Liza tapped the heated seat of his pickup and grinned like a kid on Christmas Eve. "I love seeing what they do every year. Oh, and we just have to get a piece of chocolate penuche from the Candy Counter."

Jaime found himself smiling and filled with a Christmas spirit that he hadn't experienced in a long time. Liza was infectious. "I love all of your ideas. Just tell me what to do and I'm ready to celebrate Christmas —Echo Ridge style."

"Thanks for being a good sport about the ugly sweater party. I'm so glad that you're coming with me."

"I wouldn't want to miss it," Jaime said.

"Well, you are about as far from the ugly sweater caliber as one could get," Liza replied. "You always look so good."

"Thank you. You look stylish and beautiful. I love the silver threading in your sweater."

Liza looked down at her sweater and smiled. "I love that you noticed that detail."

"I notice a lot about you that is to be admired."

Liza squeezed his hand. "Same."

There was a little black ice on the road at the base of the canyon, and Jaime slowed down as they turned onto Center Street. He parked in front of the run-down thrift shop, and Liza almost got out of the pickup before he could get her door.

"Come on. Let's go pick out ugly sweaters!" Jaime said as he helped her out of the pickup.

They made a beeline for the sweater racks and Liza pulled out a hairy sweater and started laughing. "How about this one?"

"That looks like a stuffed tabby cat," Jaime said.

Liza covered her mouth but couldn't hide the snort that escaped amidst her laughter.

Twenty minutes later, they had purchased three of the ugliest sweaters they could find.

"I'm going to add a few touches to mine, and it will be ready." Liza squeezed the bag of sweaters to her chest.

"Well, which one are you wearing?"

"Both."

Jaime furrowed his brow. "Won't you get too hot? The party is indoors."

Liza smiled. "You'll see."

"Okay, park on the street here." Liza indicated the one empty spot in front of Kenworth's.

Jaime opened her door and held tight to her hand so that she wouldn't slip on the ice in her low-heeled black boots. They walked about twenty paces to the front of the biggest window at Kenworth's.

Liza gasped and clapped her hands, her breath billowing out in frosty clouds. "It's the Christmas village patterned after Echo Ridge! I love this one." She pulled on Jaime's arm. "Look, there's Kenworth's and Chickadee Lake with the ice skaters. Oh, and there's the Emerald Inn, and they even have Fay's Café!"

Jaime followed her pointing finger, recognizing some of the places he'd visited in Echo Ridge. Liza was beaming as she chattered away. Her smile made him smile, and he stopped looking at the window display and just noticed her. She was beautiful, but it wasn't just her body; it was the light in her eyes, the vibrant music of her voice, and the way she experienced life—and all of that was only the beginning of why he was falling in love with her. Wait, could he say that? Was he really in love with her?

She turned in that moment and caught him staring, so Jaime did the only thing that seemed natural: he kissed her, and it wasn't a peck. She responded, and he put his arms around her and held her close. Could she feel his heart beating through the layers of their winter coats? When he finally released her, Liza looked up at him with a question in her eyes. The words were on the tip of his tongue, but that look made him question his own feelings.

"You're magical, Liza," he breathed. "Don't ever change."

Liza stood close to him, not moving away, and her eyes flicked to his lips. She leaned forward, and he thought that she might kiss him again. She placed a feather-light kiss on his cheek and then squeezed his hand.

"I never want to forget tonight," Jaime murmured.

Liza leaned toward him. "Then don't."

Jaime inhaled the fresh coconut scent of her hair and then bent to kiss her again. He pressed his lips to hers slowly, caressing her lower lip with his as he pulled her closer to him. Liza gave a soft sigh and threaded her fingers through his hair.

"Hey, lovebirds, better save some for tomorrow night at the party," Nita crooned. "I'll have mistletoe."

"That was perfect timing," Jaime whispered. "Weren't you just telling me how hard Nita is to convince?"

Liza nodded, and in a breathy voice she said, "I don't think she has any doubt now." When she spoke, her eyes didn't sparkle the way they had a few moments earlier.

"What's wrong?"

"Oh, nothing," Liza replied. "It's just hard to remember how to keep the act up in front of everyone."

Her words ripped open a hole in his chest. Hadn't she

felt anything in those last few moments? Jaime thought of how Alex had said he shouldn't have a girlfriend. Maybe his son knew something he didn't.

155

Chapter Twenty-Three

L iza's heart must have pumped all the blood to her lips, because her mouth still tingled where Jaime had kissed her. Oh, and his kisses were delicious. She wanted more of them. For a moment there when Jaime had first kissed her in front of the window display, she had thought he really meant it. She was about to confess that she had developed feelings for him when Nita interrupted and Jaime indicated that the kiss was the proof they needed.

That kiss wasn't an act, and if it was proof, then it was proof that he was falling in love with her. That's what Liza told herself, but she'd never have the guts to say such things to Jaime.

The bell chimed as they walked into Kenworth's, and Liza's mouth started watering immediately.

"Those chocolates smell so good. Are they the ones

you were talking about?" Jaime tilted his head toward the Candy Counter.

Liza nodded. "And it smells like they have roasted nuts tonight too. We are in luck." She tugged on Jaime's hand, and they hurried over to the Candy Counter.

Reese was working, and they chatted a few minutes about all of the snowstorms and trying to keep up with Christmas demands. Reese gave them extra-full cones of roasted nuts with toasted coconut. Liza and Jaime each selected three chocolates, and they ate slowly as they meandered through the aisles of Kenworth.

"Yummy! I love these hand-dipped chocolates." Liza savored the last mouthful of penuche.

"I'm going to have to add more to my workout routine now or else avoid Kenworth's altogether," Jaime said.

"I'd say sorry, but these are too good to apologize for." Liza crunched on the warm toasted nuts and led Jaime toward the beautiful Christmas tree centered in front of the women's department. "And here is the hope tree."

Jaime stopped and stared at the tree. Liza tried to see it through his eyes: a simple artificial tree with beautiful glass ornaments and handwritten tags hung from the branches.

They approached the tree almost reverently, and Liza started in on the tags. There were toys listed, as well as gift cards, and clothing for children and adults. Jaime carefully moved the tags so that he could read them as well.

"How about this one?" Jaime removed one of the tags from the tree and held it out to Liza.

She read it and smiled. It was a request for a twenty-dollar gift card to the Candy Counter. "That would be perfect!"

"Well, that's almost too easy," Jaime said. "I'll buy a gift card on our way out, and then do I turn it in here?"

"Yes, they like everything purchased by the twenty-third if possible." She continued sifting through the tags. There had to be nearly a hundred tags, and it gave Liza a thrill to think of how many people's lives were touched because of this one tree. Hope was delivered and received both by the giver and the recipient. She found a request for girl's snow boots, size 6, and pulled that off the tree. She remembered how excited she had been as a child when she'd received new snow boots for Christmas one year and then a storm had come through and dumped six inches of fresh powder. Everyone seemed to be on the mountain during that Christmas break.

Liza waited for Jaime to examine more of the tags, and she was touched when she saw him pull off two more. They walked around the store a little longer, and Jaime purchased the gift card from the Candy Counter, dropping it off near the hope tree before they left. All the way home, Liza kept thinking that she had picked up more hope that night for a future with Jaime.

On Saturday, Jaime showed up just before five wearing his ugly Christmas sweater. It sported a brown argyle plaid pattern, and with Liza's assistance, he had hot-glued dozens of red and green Christmas pom poms all over the sweater. He modeled his sweater to the Sorenson family and noticed that Liza had a coat on.

"Are you going to let me see your sweater or not?" he asked.

Liza wagged her finger in front of Jaime's face. "Oh no, you don't. I'm not giving you any advantages. I intend to win this contest."

"But what if they have a prize for the best ugly sweater couple?"

Liza hesitated. "You do have a point there. Okay, you win." She unzipped her coat and pulled it off to reveal the ugliest sweater Jaime had ever seen. Somehow she had taken the tabby cat sweater, cut it in half, and paired it with an equally ugly knitted Christmas tree sweater.

Jaime started laughing. "We definitely need a picture of this."

"I'll help with that." Adina pulled out her phone.

"But first, we need our hats," Liza said. She pulled out two red Santa hats with a flourish.

Jaime shook his head. "This party is for ugly sweaters, not hats."

Liza put the hat on his head and kissed his cheek. "Do you want to win or not?"

"Okay, let's win this thing." Jaime adjusted his hat and grinned at Liza as she put on her Santa hat.

"You two make the cutest couple," Adina said as she snapped a few pictures.

Jaime handed her his phone. "Take a few with mine, and I promise I won't post this anywhere until after the party is over." He looked to Liza, and she nodded.

Jaime kissed Liza's cheek in one of the pictures, and he couldn't wait to see the look on her face when he studied the photos later on. Nita's party was on the other side of town and with the snowy roads, it would take them nearly forty-five minutes to get there. Jaime was actually looking forward to the extra time he could spend talking to Liza. He remembered her sharing a desire to be a novelist, and he wanted to encourage her to trust him with her dreams. That thought served as a reminder that he didn't trust Liza enough to share the truth about his broken relationship with his son.

"What's on your mind, Jaime?" Liza peered at him from beneath the white fir trim of the Santa hat.

His thoughts snapped back to the present. Liza was beautiful, even in her ugly sweater. "You actually," he replied. "When we were in Florida you said you were writing a romance novel. Have you had time to work on it?"

Liza flexed her fingers in front of the heating vent. "I

usually try to steal a few minutes every night. It's coming along. I'm having a hard time deciding what publishing path I want to take."

"Oh? What are the choices?"

Liza explained to him how she could choose to go with a traditional publisher or step onto the indie track. "I'm leaning toward starting my own publishing company and creating my books so that I'll have full control. Saying it out loud makes me a little nervous, though."

"I bet it does," Jaime responded. "But at the same time, doesn't it give you a feeling of exhilaration? It's the way I felt when I decided to go out on my own and create my business."

"Yes, it does." Liza leaned forward in her seat, her hands resting on her knees. "You know, I never really thought of it that way. A lot of people discourage authors from self-publishing, but at the same time they encourage someone who wants to start their own business. It's an interesting dichotomy."

"Exactly. You're smart. I'm sure you've studied it out, and you're not going to jump in without doing your homework. If you think that's the best route, I'm sure you'll be successful."

"Thank you. That means a lot. I'm still not completely sure what I'll do, but I love looking at it through the lens of the business owner. I'm working so hard to create this work of art, and I want it to be well taken care of."

"I hope you let me read it when it's finished."

Liza covered her face with her hands. "That makes me even more nervous."

"Why? I like reading."

"I'm just worried about what you will think. I'm worried about what anyone will think. What if they don't like my book? What if it's one of those that you start reading and can't get past the second chapter?"

Jaime reached over and took her hand, squeezing it gently. "I've seen your work ethic in action. I'm sure anything you create will be worth more than just the first twenty pages. Don't doubt yourself. Just go after it. Create it, and don't worry about what anyone else thinks."

Liza leaned back in the seat and sighed. "That's easy to say but hard to do."

"That's why I'm qualified to say it. Can you imagine the paralysis I had to go through when starting my own business? I worried that there might be too much competition out there. I thought maybe other people could do a better job than me and I wouldn't be able to do enough business to keep afloat. But here I am. My business is more successful than I ever thought it would be when I first started three years ago."

"Okay." Liza looked at him and smiled. "I'm going to do it. I'll stop being afraid and I'll do the very best I can, and we'll see what happens."

"Spoken like a true artist." Jaime liked the way she'd

said "we'll see," as if he might be around to celebrate in her success.

"You know, you can be pretty inspiring. I might want to hang around you more often." Liza covered his hand with hers.

"Well, I'm glad you feel that way, since we are engaged." Jaime winked, and Liza giggled.

The party was a hit. Everyone laughed and cheered as each new guest entered with their ugly sweaters. Some had real lights that twinkled on sweatshirts, while others had gone the more traditional route with hideous reindeer knitted in crazy designs across the sweaters or Santas embroidered with thousands of tiny stitches. Nita had arranged for several different prizes—the ugliest sweater, the best grandma sweater, and the sweater with the most Christmas spirit were just a few of the categories.

Jaime avoided the eggnog and all other alcoholic beverages, and he sensed that Liza noticed his choices. They received several more congratulations and questions of when the big date would occur. Liza told friends they were waiting until after the holidays were over to start planning anything.

"There is enough stress getting everything ready for Christmas without having to think about planning the wedding," Liza said. "But have you seen my ring?"

Everyone loved the ring and agreed with the sentiment on wedding planning. For the most part, they didn't badger them for more details.

"Your Santa hats just make those sweaters work," Nita said. "Thank you so much for coming."

"Thanks for inviting us. This has been too much fun." Liza admired Nita's sweater—one of the light-up variety that she had seen being sold at the local discount store.

"Liza speaks very highly of you. She's lucky to have such a good friend," Jaime said.

"She's lucky to have you. I haven't seen Liza this happy in nearly a year. We're all so happy for you two."

Jaime glanced at Liza and noticed a beautiful blush spreading across her cheeks. Nita's words must've impacted her as well; she looked as happy as Jaime felt. "People have been telling me the same thing."

Liza's head jerked up, and she looked at him with a question in her eyes. He smiled at her, and her cheeks lifted in a big smile. It was as close to the truth as he could get for now.

The party started winding down around eleven, and Jaime caught a case of the yawns as they were heading out. "Hey, do you mind if I stop at the gas station for treats? This time of year, I always feel tired earlier, like I'm a bear looking for a place to hibernate."

"I don't mind. Let's go."

They stopped at the gas station and fueled up. Jaime grabbed a medium-sized bag of Nacho Cheese Doritos and a large fountain drink of the Diet Cherry Coke variety.

"So is it always Cherry Coke, or do you venture out and mix flavors?" Liza asked.

"Pretty much always Cherry Coke. You want some?"

Liza wrinkled her nose. "Not a huge fan of cherry, but I love Doritos."

"Well, it's a good thing this isn't a snack size bag. I'm happy to share."

Liza stood next to him as they paid. "Are you sure you don't want to get anything else?"

"No thank you. I ate too much of Nita's sweet Chex mix. Did you taste those sugar cookies?"

Jaime nodded and closed his eyes. "Those were so tender. We need to get that recipe."

"I think it was Nita's cousin who brought them. I bet I can track it down."

"If you want to move the wedding up, I guess we could make sugar cookies for refreshments."

"Quit teasing me." Liza bumped him with her hip, and Jaime laughed.

They hurried back to the pickup and laughed when they both hit the buttons to turn on the seat heaters.

"I'm still kind of bummed that we didn't win the couples contest," Jaime said. "Especially since everyone kept saying how good we look together." Liza had won the most creative Christmas sweater award, but Jaime hadn't won anything.

"It's your fault," Liza said.

"Mine? Why?" Jaime pointed at his sweater. "This thing is terrible."

"But the person wearing it is so gorgeous that it just doesn't look as ugly as it should."

Jaime chuckled and turned away to hide the warmth he felt in his cheeks. "You only won because it's such a stark contrast. Beauty to ashes, you know."

"Hmm. I like that, Romeo."

"Good, but I'm not going to call you Juliet, because our story should have a better ending, don't you think?"

Liza leaned back in her seat. "Definitely."

Jaime liked the way she'd agreed so readily. He also liked how comfortable he felt with her riding in his pickup. It didn't feel like they were pretending at all.

Chapter Twenty-Four

❧

"You can go ahead and open the chips," Jaime said.

Liza pulled open the bag and inhaled the smell of salty, cheesy goodness. She pulled out a chip and popped it in her mouth whole, enjoying the delicious crunch. She held the chip bag over the console in the middle so that Jaime could easily reach in for chips as he drove. "So how is our story going to end?" she asked.

"You mean the breakup?"

"Yeah, I was thinking this could be really awkward. You're my friend, and if you're my ex, how can we still be friends?"

"Dang. That's a good point." Jaime took another chip from the bag and ate it in three careful bites. "Could we say that we decided we're better friends than lovers?"

"That sounds so lame." And it definitely wasn't the truth. Liza could never say that after having been kissed by Jaime. Even now, when she thought of the way he kissed her in front of Kenworth's window display, her lips still tingled.

"We could send Mark to Costa Rica and have my parents take him out on a deep-sea fishing expedition and use him as bait." Jaime turned to her in all seriousness.

"Jaime! You're killing me."

"No, I'm killing Mark. We should've done that first. It would've saved us a lot of trouble."

Liza laughed. "Well, I guess we have time to think about it. But since I'm a writer, I keep wondering how the story will end."

"Don't all good stories have a twist near the end?" Jaime arched an eyebrow and gave her a devilish grin.

Liza put a hand over her stomach as if to hold in the hummingbirds; they definitely weren't butterflies anymore. "I really like spending time with you. These past couple weeks have made me feel really happy."

"And hopefully they've given you great ideas for that romance you're writing. In fact, if you'd like, we could practice a few more kisses so you'll be able to accurately describe them in your book."

Liza reached over and pushed Jaime's shoulder. "You'd better stop teasing me."

Jaime reached his hand in the bag of chips. "Hey, did you eat all of those Doritos already?"

"No, we ate them. I shared with you. I've been holding the bag the whole time."

"Shared?" Jaime lifted his eyebrows and shook his head. "I think I ate seven chips."

Liza looked into the empty bag. They'd been talking, and she hadn't been paying attention to how many chips she had eaten. "Oops, sorry. They are a guilty pleasure of mine."

Jaime pretended to sulk. "I can usually nurse a bag of Doritos for an hour. The crunch keeps me awake."

"Well, I can keep you awake." Liza waggled her eyebrows and giggled when Jaime widened his eyes.

"I thought you had to get home so you could be up early in the morning for church."

"I do, but I'm feeling good because I just ate more than half of a pint-size bag of chips."

"More than half?" Jaime scoffed. "How many servings are in one bag?"

Liza scanned the label. "Three? These companies have never seen anyone eat Doritos before."

Jaime tapped the steering wheel. "So you ate two-thirds of the bag."

"Well, next time you should count out the chips, General Dorito." Liza wadded up the bag and threw it at him.

Jaime laughed. "You're fun. I like your sass."

"Good," Liza said, "because it's not going anywhere."

"Unlike my chips." Jaime leaned toward his window to keep Liza from pulling on his ear.

"At least one problem is solved because of all of this," Liza said.

"What's that?"

"I know what to get you for Christmas." She gave him a smug grin and guzzled some of his Diet Cherry Coke.

They bantered back and forth, and the time passed much more quickly than it would have alone. Liza almost wished they could keep driving, but she didn't want to be drowsy during Pastor Louis's sermon on Sunday.

The temperature continued to drop as they drove up the mouth of Echo Ridge Canyon. Jaime zipped up his coat and walked Liza up to her doorstep. "Thanks again for another wonderful evening. When will I see you next?"

"After work on Monday? Unless you have another Christmas function before then."

"Unfortunately, I don't, but let's go to dinner Monday. Just to keep appearances up."

Liza nodded. "Good thinking. It's a plan."

Jaime kissed her cheek. "Good night, Liza."

"Good night." Liza walked into the house and hung her coat in the closet quietly. Her parents must've gone to bed early, which was good, because they would definitely razz her about the glow that surely showed in her eyes. She was in love with Jaime. He was everything that Mark had never been. Jaime was better than the guy from her dreams, because she hadn't even thought to dream of all the qualities that he had. They got along so well, conversed so naturally, and laughed a lot.

Liza looked at the calendar. It was December thirteenth. There were less than twelve days left until Christmas, and for once she wasn't looking forward to it, because it signaled the beginning of the end of her relationship with Jaime.

Sunday afternoon, Kori called and as soon as Jaime saw her name on the ID, he prepared to record the conversation. He said hello and pushed the record feature to gather evidence of Kori's imminent harassment. She only called when she was upset about something.

"You are such a piece of scum!" she screeched. "Why are you doing this?"

"Doing what?"

"Faking an engagement to put on a good face for the court!"

"What do you mean?" It was hard to keep his voice even while his mind went on high-alert wondering how Kori had heard the news.

"Don't pretend that you don't know. Your secret's out. You thought I'd miss the pictures in my feed of her and that huge ring? Why are you doing this to Alex?"

"I am not doing anything to Alex. I talked to him

about dating and helped reassure him since you obviously gave him some false information. Dating is normal after a divorce."

"Yeah, dating. Not engaged to be married!"

"Well, that usually happens after you date someone," Jamie said.

"You think you can just throw your family away? You are such a loser!"

Jaime took a deep breath and remembered to separate himself from Kori's drama as she continued to call him names, threaten him, and insult him. "Besides calling to insult me, did you need anything?"

Kori told him where to go and promptly hung up the phone.

Jaime stepped outside and sucked in a wintry breath of air, allowing the frigid December breeze to clear his head and suck away the emotions that Kori was so adept at eliciting. He wouldn't gloat over this latest piece of evidence, but it was another nail in the coffin that Kori was building herself each day.

Jaime had kept careful record of their correspondence as well as reports of her treatment toward Alex for the past year—mostly things that Alex wasn't aware of, like why his meds always disappeared when he was around his mother. In addition, Jaime had written the letter to the judge, and Jared was getting ready to submit it along with other evidence purporting that Jaime was a qualified guardian for Alex and Kori should be placed under scrutiny.

Shivering, he stepped back inside, shrugged off the remnants of his former life, and decided to be proactive. Jaime took a few minutes to send an email to Alex inviting him to come and visit during the Christmas break. Then he looked online to find the perfect gift for a fourteen-year-old, which apparently didn't exist. He finally settled on a desk lamp with a charging station and a year-long subscription to Spotify. Alex hardly ever took out his earbuds when he'd been at home. For the longest time, Jaime thought it was just because he loved loud music like other teenagers, but now he realized that Alex was probably trying to drown out the fighting.

Jaime wanted to feel excited about the efforts he had made to reconnect with Alex, but they might as well have been standing on opposite sides of the Grand Canyon for the response he'd received. He made a mental note to think of something meaningful he could do for Alex. Perhaps if he wrote him a letter and recounted some of the good memories he had of his time with Alex, it might comfort his son and help him realize that there was good despite the bad in his life. He wished that he could tell Alex all about Liza to convey the truth that there was good despite the bad.

Jaime put his head in his hands. After he'd gotten over the initial shock of having to extend the fake engagement, he'd been surprised with the realization that it could be a benefit to him, and he'd pursued it. But now, he wished more than ever that he could tell Liza about Alex. He felt so ashamed in that moment. His own son didn't even want to see him during Christmas. When he finally told Liza the truth, she would learn just how terrible a father he was—his own son couldn't stand to be around him. Every time he thought about what the truth would mean, he wondered if it would just be better to let Liza go quietly out of his life. But his heart rebelled at those thoughts because he loved Liza. Loving her was worth figuring out how to show her all his flaws. He just didn't know how to do it.

Chapter Twenty-Five

On Monday, when Liza went into work, Rick was waiting for her and ushered her into his office. "Mark Pratt tells me he's been trying to get a hold of you, but his calls aren't going through. Do you know why that's the case?"

Liza clenched her jaw and forced herself to take a deep breath before answering him. "Rick, I don't take business calls on my personal cell phone. If Mark wants to reach me, then he needs to call me during office hours. I haven't received any messages here at work."

Rick wrinkled his brow and looked down at her. "Well, why don't you give him a call today?"

"I'd rather not work with Mark directly. He indicated that he needs services that are above my pay level."

Rick grinned. "What a perfect way to show your qualifications for the promotion you want so badly."

"And when will the promotion happen?" Liza was sick and tired of playing this game with Rick every time he wanted her to do something that wasn't in her job description. He kept dangling the carrot of a promotion in front of her face. It was time for his manipulation to stop.

Rick leaned back on his desk. "You call Mark, figure out what he needs and what we need to do to get this project going, and then we'll talk."

Liza folded her arms and stood up straight. "I'll give Mark a call, but I want you to know that I refuse to work with anyone who harasses me, and that's what I have experienced from Mark in the past."

"He assured me that he'd be on his best behavior—business only. Please, Liza?"

The way Rick asked made Liza swallow her retort. "Fine."

"That's what I like to hear."

She shrugged off Rick's parting words as she went back to her desk.

She picked up the phone and dialed Mark's cell phone number, which she still had memorized. Unfortunately, he answered with a cheerful hello.

"Hi, this is Liza from Stellar Ads. Rick told me that you were trying to reach me about a project for your office."

"Liza, it's so good to hear your voice. How are things

going with the wedding plans?" His voice was syrupy sweet, but the nasal quality was still there.

"Mark, this is a business call only. If you aren't ready, then I suggest you call the office back at a later time."

"A little testy today, are we? Well, I really don't work well over the phone. I'd like to know if you can come out to my office and meet with me so we can go over designs and do a little editing on what I have started so far."

"Absolutely not. I work from my office, and any clients who are serious don't have a problem here. We have a lovely conference room, and I'm sure that Rick would be happy to sit in if you'd like his input." Liza struggled to keep her voice low and even.

"I'll just run it by Rick. I have the feeling that when I present it to him, he'll agree it's best if you came to my office."

He was right, and Liza knew it, because a master manipulator like Mark always managed to get people to do things they otherwise wouldn't. She had to put a stop to this now. "Mark. This is inappropriate behavior and has nothing to do with your business or Stellar Ads. Working with me is not going to change my feelings about you. I am engaged to marry Jaime."

"The way I see it, until you are married, you're still available and could change your mind."

Liza hung up the phone. She was seething, and her neck and face were probably the same shade as the holly berries that dotted the wreath in the office. Her fingers shook, and she felt herself going back to that place that Mark had taken her so many times. "Not again."

What would Jaime tell her to do? She blew out a breath and inhaled slowly, filling up her lungs. Jaime would tell her that she was stronger than Mark's manipulation. Jaime would tell her not to let Mark steal any more of her energy. Liza nodded and took three more deep breaths. Her hands weren't trembling anymore, but she craved the look of comfort she knew she'd find in Jaime's soft green eyes.

It was nearly a quarter after five when Liza finally left the office. She waved at Andy Edwards as he helped his dad with boxes going into Pop's shipping and wondered if she should change careers. Holiday shipping was a nightmare, but maybe not the same kind she worked in every day. Liza flipped the radio station to one with all Christmas songs and hummed as she drove to Jaime's house. She didn't really have a reason to go there and they both knew that, yet he'd invited her to come by. He'd even texted her after lunch to see if she was still planning to stop. Liza felt giddy when she remembered the moment the text had come in—the feeling that someone like Jaime wanted to see her.

His place still looked like the front of a Christmas greeting card with the white fence draped in snow contrasted against the backdrop of so many tall ever-greens. Liza hurried up the steps, watching for spots of ice, and knocked on the door. Jaime had added a Christmas wreath and wrapped the railing with red ribbon last week. He had a few sparse decorations in his home and no Christmas tree, but he was trying to invite the Christmas spirit. Jaime opened the door, the wreath swinging as he did so.

Liza hugged him as she came inside. "Your house looks a little bit more like Christmas every day," she told him.

"Thanks." He hesitated only a fraction of a second before hugging her back.

"It's so good to see you," Liza murmured.

"I agree." Jaime stepped back, eyeing her carefully. "Everything okay at work today?"

Liza's shoulders slumped. "Not quite."

Jaime took her coat. "Come have some hot cocoa and tell me all about it."

Liza filled him in on Rick's demands, his proposed promotion, and the ensuing conversation with Mark. "It just keeps getting worse instead of better. I thought having a fiancé would get him off my back, but he's more determined than ever."

"I think you handled it very well. I definitely don't think you should talk to him or meet with him in person."

"I won't work with him. But for some reason, he's

gotten under Rick's skin and cast a spell on him. I'm afraid I will lose my job if I refuse to work with Mark."

Jaime frowned. "I know that puts you in a bad position, but if Rick won't honor your request, then he doesn't deserve to have you work for him."

"I looked again for job openings during my lunch break today. There aren't many available in Echo Ridge that have anything to do with writing."

"What about your book? How close are you to finishing it?" Jaime handed her a mug of cocoa.

"I am getting close, but with edits and cover design and then typesetting, I'm still at least two or three months away from having a final product."

Jaime sipped his cocoa and looked out the window. "So, what if you took a part-time job and were able to do some freelancing on the side while you finish your novel?"

"That's a great idea." Liza brightened, but then she leaned back against the chair. "But I'm worried that I couldn't get my income to the level I'm at now, and that puts my parents in a bind as well. I know they wouldn't require me to pay rent money if I didn't have it, but I really wanted to prove to myself that I could be independent."

Jaime nodded. "I have a friend who runs an online magazine. She's always looking for new submissions. I wonder if you might be able to write anything that would suit her tastes."

"What kind of a magazine?"

"Something like country living or small-town communities. I can't think of the title right now, but I'll look it up."

"Are you serious? I could totally write for a magazine like that." Liza felt the stirrings of hope in her chest. Maybe Jaime was right. "If I started now, then maybe I could get enough built up to last through the holiday season. I'm sure I can find a way to put off Mark and Rick at least that long."

"Yes, I'll get you her contact info and anything else I can think of."

"Thanks, Jaime. You always have a way of making me feel better."

"Ah, it's just the hot cocoa today." He winked.

They lingered over their hot cocoa and ended up having eggs and toast for dinner. It was nine thirty by the time she left his place, and even then, she wished she didn't have to go.

"Thanks so much for dinner," she said, "and especially the good advice."

"My pleasure." Jaime put his hand on her back as they walked slowly to the front door.

"Let's pray that Mark hasn't already contacted Rick. I hope I can make it through the holidays with my job."

Jaime pulled her close and nuzzled her neck. "It's okay. I promise that it's going to be okay."

"How?"

"I guess if we have to fake a marriage, then we will," he said, but he sounded like he was only half joking.

"No, I've put you through enough with a fake engagement, but thank you." Liza hugged him. "Your strength has helped me so much."

As soon as the door closed, Jaime felt Liza's absence and wished that he could open the door and call her back inside. He loved being with her. He felt like he'd only been half living until he'd met Liza. He hadn't craved a drink or felt depressed since she'd run into him. Things were going so well with his business that he had hired another part-time position with plans to bring that employee on full-time. He was saving up a nice nest egg for an expensive court battle if it came to that.

Kori had blown up his phone with all kinds of incriminating texts, and he continued to collect the information needed. He seemed to be winning on that front, but he was losing with his son. Alex hadn't responded to his invitations to visit during Christmas break. He was supposed to see him this coming weekend, and he thought about inviting Liza to travel to Alex's school on Saturday. He was planning to invite her tonight, but when she'd arrived, he'd seen the distress in her eyes. He made yet another excuse not to tell her the truth, but he didn't feel as guilty as he had in the past. Liza had really needed him, and they had come up with some great possible solutions for her.

He thought again of the words they'd exchanged when she'd said goodbye. She'd mentioned the fake engagement. He smiled when he thought of all that had come because of the pretend relationship. In that moment, he was struck with a thought: Why did this have to be a fake engagement? And then he remembered Alex and Kori, and he shivered. Would Liza forgive him when he finally told her the truth?

Chapter Twenty-Six

❧

Liza felt so much better the next morning that she sang Christmas carols all the way to work. She happily typed up details for upcoming projects and sped through the copy edits needed on the next batch of web advertisements.

It was a few minutes before ten when she received a message from Rick requesting her presence in his office. The wheels of her chair squeaked as she scooted out from her desk. Her nerves felt squeaky too as she recalled the way she'd ended the call with Mark the day before. She wasn't naïve enough to believe that he would let things lie. She rolled her shoulders back and prepared for the coming onslaught.

Rick motioned for her to come in when she rapped on the side of his door. He finished typing and then leaned back, folding his arms over his beefy middle.

"Liza, I'm very concerned about what's happening with you and Mark Pratt. There seems to be some sort of miscommunication."

Rick's terse voice pricked at the edges of a headache threatening to take over her frontal lobe. "I'm not sure what you mean."

"Mark really wants to meet with you, and I'm getting mixed messages. He said he thinks that you will be the best candidate for the job that he needs done. Do you have a problem working with him?"

Liza rolled her shoulders back. "Rick, I told you before that I don't want to work with Mark. He is manipulative, and the only reason he's interested in our company is because he wants to ingratiate himself into my life."

"Well, I'm not seeing that," Rick said. "Can you do this job or not, Liza?"

This was the moment she'd hoped to avoid for another month or two. Liza thought about the discussion she'd had with Jaime the night before. She'd been so sure of herself then, especially when they discussed the many options she had. Right now, staring at Rick the Prick, she couldn't see those options clearly—what she could see was her job hanging by a thread.

"Liza?" The impatience in Rick's voice was barely veiled.

He was really no different from Mark. That was the point that she'd been missing all along. She didn't have to work with Mark, and she didn't have to work with Rick either. "No. I guess I can't." Liza's tone was even, belying a strength that was tenuous at best. She took in a breath and blurted out, "So do whatever you need to, but I'm not working with Mark Pratt."

There were two beats of silence, and then Rick cleared his throat. "You're fired. Clean out your desk and go home."

"Thank you," Liza said. She was rewarded with a stunned look before she turned and walked quickly from his office. Liza bit her lip as she walked back to her desk. She grabbed a box from the copy center, and within five minutes she had deposited all her belongings inside.

She was just about to pick up the box when Nita rushed into her cubicle. "What are you doing? You are not leaving!"

Liza turned to her friend, and she could feel the tears stinging the edges of her eyes. "Don't," she whispered. "I have to keep it together. We can talk later. I'll be okay."

Nita stepped closer and pulled Liza into a fierce hug. "This isn't the end."

With a nod, Liza picked up her purse, slung it on her shoulder, and hefted the box. She walked out of the office without glancing to the left or the right and set the box on top of her car. She clenched her jaw as she unlocked the door and put the box into the back seat.

She waited until she pulled away from the building and was on Main Street before allowing the tears to fall.

But even then, she couldn't let them come full force or she'd get in another wreck. That made her think of Jaime. He would know what to do. Would he think she was a basket case, showing up at his door every day with her problems?

Liza was headed home anyway, and she would have to pass by his house. Even though the situation she was in wasn't likely to change, she still yearned for his wisdom, his comfort, and his love. Yes, his love, because that was the only way she could describe the feelings they shared. Losing her job had forced clarity to her perspective, and she was going to tell Jaime how she really felt about him today. If he rejected her, she had nothing left to lose and could go home and have the pity party to end all pity parties.

Liza maneuvered carefully through the icy roads and pulled into Jaime's driveway. She leaned forward and rested her head against the steering wheel. The sob she'd been holding in found its way out. She wasn't necessarily even crying for the loss of her job. She was crying because she'd finally taken a stand and she was ... relieved.

She took in a shaky breath and opened her car door. That was when she noticed the other car in the driveway. Noodles! Jaime was probably meeting with a client. She was debating whether to wait in her car or slip into his kitchen and wait there when the front door opened. A gorgeous woman with golden tresses glided down the steps. When she saw Liza, she looked like a tiger about to pounce. Liza didn't have time to react before the woman was standing in front of her. The woman didn't look beautiful close up; she looked angry and worn. Liza stood, holding onto the doorframe for support.

"You think you have some prize, huh?" the woman spat. "Jaime is a great actor, and you're dumb enough to fall for him."

"Oh, wait. You must be Kori." Liza spoke into the frigid air and wondered if this woman was related to the ice queen.

Kori narrowed her eyes. "Jaime is engaged to you so he'll look good in front of the judge. He wants more time with Alex so he won't have to pay as much in child support. Being engaged to Miss Goody Two-Shoes makes it appear as if his bad-boy drinking days are over. But I'm smarter than that." She pointed at Liza. "You don't know what you're doing. I was a good wife, and he didn't want me. When he's through using you, he'll throw you away too."

Liza opened her mouth, but there were no words. Her mind was under attack as she tried to process all the words spewing from Kori's mouth. None of it made sense, but she couldn't ask this crazy woman questions. Instead, she pushed past Kori and hurried up the steps to Jaime's front door. She opened it and went inside without knocking.

"Kori, I told you to leave." Jaime's voice was gruff as he approached the entryway.

"It's me," Liza whispered.

"Oh gosh, I'm sorry." Jaime stopped when he saw her face. "Hey, are you all right? It looks like you've been crying. What's wrong?"

Liza lifted a hand to her eyes and felt a smudge of mascara. She'd already forgotten about Rick and how upset she'd been to lose her job. That was a minor event compared to what was happening right now.

"How can I help?" Jaime put his arms around her and hugged her. He moved to kiss her.

Liza held up her hand. There was no way she could kiss him now. "Wait. Who is Alex?"

Jaime's eyes widened and he stepped back. "Alex? How did you —"

"Kori was just leaving when I arrived. From what she said, it sounds like Alex is your son."

Jaime looked up at the ceiling and shook his head. "This isn't how I wanted to tell you."

"Oh, so you were going to wait, what, another month, another year before telling me that you had a son?" The sting of betrayal took Liza's breath away. A sob welled up in her throat, and when she spoke, her voice was strained. "You lied to me."

Jaime held his hands out in front of him with a pleading expression on his face. "No, I never intended to keep Alex a secret, but things were complicated and then I didn't know how to tell you."

"What kind of a father pretends he doesn't have a son? I have seen you nearly every day since we met, and there's no sign of Alex in your life."

A pained expression crossed Jaime's face. "Alex is away at boarding school. You wouldn't believe what I had to go through to get him there. But I was willing to do anything to save him from Kori."

"Boarding school?" Liza studied Jaime. He sounded sincere, but it still didn't make sense. "I don't understand why you couldn't tell me that you have a son."

"Don't you remember the conversation we had about boarding school? In your opinion, I'm some kind of monster for sending my son there and he'll turn out to be a snob."

Liza paused. She had said those things about Chrissy at work, but that had been on their way home from Florida. "Jaime, you'd already spent an entire weekend with me by that point and never mentioned your son. Don't try to pin this on me."

"I'm sorry. I just—"

"How old is he?" Liza demanded.

"He's fourteen." Jaime stuffed his hands in his pockets. "He's a great kid and is doing so much better since he's been away at school."

Liza's ears were ringing as she tried to sort out what Jaime was telling her. He had a teenager! He had deceived her again, and this was much more serious than hiding the fact that he had a DUI. She tried to slow things down in her mind, but there were too many pieces scattering every which way. "Jaime, I don't know what game you're playing here, but I do know one thing. We agreed that we would be honest with each other. That was back when we were just friends. I thought we were more than that, and this really hurts."

Jaime stepped forward. "Let me try to help you understand."

"No, I understand that I made a mistake. We started this relationship on false pretenses, so I don't know why I thought it could change to something real. I have to go." She turned and hurried out the door.

His feet pounded down the steps behind her. "Liza, wait! Please don't leave like this."

But Liza had to leave. She had to run. She got in her car and sped away as quickly as she could. When she arrived home, she drove around back and sat in her car and sobbed. Her phone rang and Jaime's handsome face showed up on her screen, but she rejected the call. When her phone started chiming with incoming texts, she silenced it and shoved it down in her purse.

When Liza couldn't cry anymore, she made her way into the house, where her mom was working in the kitchen, baking homemade bread.

"Liza, honey, what's wrong?"

She burst into tears again and told her mom everything.

"A fake engagement, Liza?" Her mom gathered her into her arms. "Oh honey, I'm so sorry it came to this."

"I made a mess of my life. I've been so stupid," Liza cried.

"You're right—it is a mess. Pretending to be engaged is not a game, but I can see why you felt like it was a good option, even if it wasn't the best choice." Mom patted her shoulder and stepped back to look her in the eye. "But as far as Jaime, I'm not sure you have all the pieces to this puzzle. The behavior you're describing just doesn't add up to what I see in him."

"But Mom, he pretended he didn't have a son!"

Her mom nodded. "And if it meant protecting you, I would do the same thing. What did you think when you met Jaime's ex-wife? Is he making everything up?"

Liza sniffed. "No, she seemed totally crazy, especially to come up to a complete stranger and say the things that she did. She looked so angry and ... sad."

Mom went back to working on the mound of bread dough. "In my experience, people go through all sorts of hard trials in their lives, but it doesn't have to break them. I've seen people mistreated, abused, and nearly broken, but they kept on going. And there's something I have observed that's really important."

"What's that?"

"Those folks who are angry and bitter often end up

letting those feelings wreck their lives. The people who sink down into a swamp of negative emotions never come back. The ones who keep their chin up, try to smile despite the hardships, and keep working—those are the ones who make it."

An image of Kori's angry face flashed through Liza's mind. "That woman seemed unstable."

Mom arranged the bread into loaf pans. "Did she seem like someone who would do just about anything to hurt Jaime? To hurt the man she used to love?"

Liza pushed down the cuticles around her fingertips. "Yeah, that's probably how I would describe her."

"Is that how you would describe Jaime?"

"No. I would describe Jaime as a man who is only honest when it suits him. A man who is willing to hide the truth and deceive when that suits him."

Mom washed her hands off in the sink, dried them on a dishcloth, and put her arm around Liza. "It's okay to be angry at him for a little while. But then you have to sort out what's really going on. Don't be too hard on yourself, and don't be too hard on him until you're certain you understand. Find out why he lied—not to justify it, but to understand."

"But, Mom, he lied to me!"

Her mom nodded slowly. "Yes, he did and you lied to us, to everyone about your engagement."

Liza opened her mouth, but there were no words to respond. Her mother was right. How was she any different than Jaime? "I'm going to go in my room and lie down."

Mom let her go, and Liza was grateful for a mother who understood when people needed their space. She curled up to her body pillow and wiped at the tears that kept flowing.

A little over an hour ago, she'd thought the worst thing that could happen to her today was losing her job, but now she knew that a broken heart was much worse. Her heart felt like it had shattered into jagged pieces that poked and dug at her soul.

Chapter Twenty-Seven

Jaime paced back and forth in his living room. He was a fool! He had known he was taking a risk when he kept Alex a secret, but he'd convinced himself it was the right thing to do. He was an idiot! Liza was the best thing that had ever happened to him. She had run into his life in the very moment he needed her. In the days leading up to the car accident, Jaime had prayed for the first time in years. He had asked God to help him know what to do, and when his pleas seemed to be met with silence, he had asked God to show him that he was loved. Liza ran into him the next morning.

Jaime had asked for evidence of God's love, and he'd received it. Then he'd messed it all up. There had to be something he could do.

That was when he noticed the time. It was only three o'clock in the afternoon. Why wasn't Liza at work? Had she stopped by to surprise him? Would she have gone back to work now?

Jaime wasn't going to wait around to find out. He jogged out to his pickup and headed toward Main Street. Snow was still piled up along the roadways, and more snow was predicted in the ten-day forecast. Echo Ridge would definitely have a white Christmas, but if Jaime couldn't fix things with Liza, then all he'd be getting was a lump of coal.

Stellar Ads had the main windows frosted and decorated with Christmas stockings and snowmen. Jaime imagined that the tall, fat snowman in the middle was patterned after Rick. He pushed through the doors, ignored the secretary, and wound his way around the wall of cubicles, but he couldn't see Liza anywhere. Finally, he turned a corner and found Nita. "Where's Liza?"

Nita looked up and her eyes filled with tears. "Oh dear. She hasn't told you yet."

"What?"

Nita sniffed and stood slowly. "Liza got fired today. She was very upset."

Jaime felt like he'd been doused in a bucket of ice water. "What? Why?" Liza had come to his house for support, and instead she'd discovered what a crummy liar her fiancé was.

Nita clenched her hands into fists. "Rick insisted that she work with Mark on a project. She refused, so he fired her."

"I'm gonna kill him," Jaime seethed.

"Probably shouldn't say things like that around here," Nita whispered. "You'll be hired as a hit man by day's end."

"That's why she came by my place." Jaime put his hand on his forehead and pushed it through his hair. "My ex was there, and she told Liza a bunch of stuff—some that I was hoping to have a chance to tell her."

"Uh-oh." Nita stood up. "That doesn't sound good. What were you hiding from her besides your DUI?"

"You know about that?" Jaime said, and then he waved his hand. "Never mind. Everyone knows about that."

"But what don't they know about?" Nita asked, putting a hand on her hip.

Jaime looked down at the floor and whispered. "That I have a son. I didn't want him to get hurt, so I kept him a secret. I realize how bad that looks now."

"You think?" Nita narrowed her eyes. "You're her fiancé!"

Jaime swallowed back his retort about being a fake fiancé, because that wasn't the truth he wanted to defend. "I love Liza. I didn't mean to hurt her. What can I do?"

"Tell her the truth, for starters," Nita said.

"I did. I've told her everything now except the reason that I had to keep my son a secret. She left before I could explain and I didn't even know about her getting fired. I wonder if she went home."

"I wouldn't go there," Nita said. "She'll need time to cool down, but I would call Adina and double-check."

Ugh. That was going to be the most uncomfortable phone call in the history of the telephone. "Okay, I'll do that. Would you mind texting me if you hear from her?"

Nita pursed her lips. "I guess. I need to chat with her first to see what's really going on."

"I get that. I wouldn't trust me either."

Nita pulled out her phone. "What's your number?"

Jaime told her and then said, "Please, if you have any sway, will you tell Liza that I really do love her? It's not an act."

"Well, you'd have to be a pretty good actor to get that sheen in your eyes just now when you were professing your love." Nita raised her eyebrows. "But that doesn't mean that I'm not considering where to punch you because you hurt my friend."

"I messed up, but seriously, if you knew the whole story, I think you'd go a tiny bit easier on me."

"We'll see," Nita replied. "And everyone will see, 'cause that's the thing about the truth. It always comes out."

As Jaime left the office of Stellar Ads, he thought about what Nita had said. The truth didn't always come out, though. There were things that he would never know about Kori and her dishonest manipulation, but he didn't want to know those things. If people thought Kori was wonderful, so be it. But Liza—she was his whole life, and somehow he needed to prove it to her. That was the truth that needed to come out—that Jaime hadn't been pretending. He really wanted to be Liza's fiancé; more than that, he wanted to be in her life forever.

Chapter Twenty-Eight

"Honey, are you sure you want to do this?" Mom said as she helped Liza load her suitcase into the car.

"I have to." Liza threw in an oversized bag and her lunch bag. She'd turned off her phone two days ago and slept most of the last twenty-four hours, but she couldn't hide anymore.

"Jaime came by again this morning," Mom said. "He truly looks like his heart is broken. Aunt Mary said she won't be offended if you change your mind."

"Good." Liza unwrapped her scarf and threw it on the passenger seat. Her aunt Mary only lived two and a half hours away, on the other side of Albany. Liza had wanted to go farther to visit Lori, but her sister lived in Buffalo and they had worse snowstorms than Echo Ridge. With the crazy winter storms predicted, she didn't dare. Her father would've tied her to a chair if he could to keep her from making this trip as it was.

"I don't think you really mean that, but even if you do, please don't stay away too long." Mom hugged Liza and patted her hair. "I'm sorry this hurts so much. I still think you need to give Jaime a chance to explain what he was thinking."

"Mom, he had so many chances. We were together every day." Liza tucked a strand of hair behind her ear. "He could have told me a thousand times. I opened my heart and soul to him." The familiar burn in the back of her throat signaled tears that Liza didn't want to cry. "I have to go, but I'll call you at the halfway point."

A few minutes later, Liza had circumvented the town of Echo Ridge, leaving behind all the places she'd pointed out to Jaime in the window display at Kenworth's. She thought back to that night. It had been perfect, and for a moment, she had seen a future here with Jaime. One where they could take their children to Chickadee Lake for ice skating and go up to Ruby Mountain Resort for skiing after downing shakes and fries at Chip's diner, or even better, pizza at Jack's. She wanted to join the library board and be part of the planning committee for the city, but now all of that seemed like wasted dreams.

Part of the reason Liza wanted to visit Aunt Mary was to check out potential jobs in Albany and maybe even visit a few companies before everything shut down for Christmas. She was running away because there was no sense in standing still and letting life beat the last breaths out of her. For a second, she thought of Jaime and all the times he'd comforted her, made her laugh, and encouraged her to go after her dreams. That was gone now.

She didn't want to cry anymore, but her tears kept pushing forth. Liza tried to concentrate on the Christmas songs on the radio, but they all reminded her of what she'd lost. By the time she arrived at Aunt Mary's, Liza was exhausted.

Mary met her at the door and enveloped her in a hug. She was older than Liza's mom by about ten years, and her face was creased with lines from her perpetual smile. "Darling, I'm so sorry about all of this," she murmured. "But don't you worry. You go right in and lie down for a while. We'll talk later."

Liza hiccupped over a sob. "Thank you."

True to her word, Aunt Mary didn't pressure Liza for explanations or details. She gave her plenty of time to relax and invited Liza to help in holiday preparations. Mary's daughter, Christina, was coming from Alabama to visit with her family on December twenty-second. Liza helped Mary clean the house, decorate, and prepare Christmas pies and cookie dough for the festivities.

On Sunday, Liza attended Mass with her aunt and felt soothed by the music and the prayers. On the way back to Mary's house, Liza patted her aunt's hand. "Thank you for letting me hide away for a few days. This was just what I needed."

"You know you're welcome to stay here," Mary said. "But I know your mother would about tan my hide if I didn't send you back home to her."

Liza smiled. "I promised her I'd be back for Christmas. I checked the weather and there is another storm coming through on Tuesday, so I think I should head back tomorrow."

"That sounds sensible. There will be just enough time for you to help me bake my Christmas cake," Mary said with a twinkle in her eye.

They returned to Mary's house, and Liza noticed a missed call from Nita. She bit her lip, considering how to proceed.

When she'd first arrived in Albany, Liza had deleted all of Jaime's texts and sent him one message.

Please do not contact me again.

She'd cried when she'd sent it, but Jaime respected her wish and didn't send any more texts. She vacillated each day between calling him to find out why he had lied or blocking his number completely. She didn't want to block Jaime from her life. She just wanted to understand why he couldn't be honest with her. But it all hurt too much to try to sort it out right now.

But she couldn't ignore everyone, so Liza called Nita back, eager to talk to her best friend.

"Liza, it's like you dropped off the face of the earth. I miss you!"

"I had to get away. I knew if I stayed there, I wouldn't have the space that I need to think about what happened. Jaime's my neighbor, so it's inevitable that I would see him."

"Oh, so you don't ever want to see him again?" Nita asked.

"No, that's the thing that is so confusing. I miss him, but at the same time I'm so angry and hurt. I feel betrayed." Liza sat in the overstuffed chair next to the window in Mary's guest room. "I want to see him, but I don't."

"That makes sense even though it doesn't," Nita replied. "Do you think it'd be worth it to at least talk to him and find out more about his son?"

"You mean so that I can justify his reason for lying?" Liza could hear the edge to her tone.

"Maybe. We all do stupid things, and at the time it seems like a good idea, or else we wouldn't do them, right?"

"Nita, I don't know. I don't know if my heart can take it if I give him another chance and then he breaks it."

"And what if he's the one? How would your heart take it if you missed out on love?"

Liza sighed. "If only my track record wasn't so horrible. I've lost confidence in myself. I've made some really bad decisions."

"I don't think you can say that, Liza. You made decisions to trust people, and because they're human, they've made mistakes. That hurts no matter who you are, but what makes the difference is if they're willing to change. If they're willing to trust you enough to be honest."

Liza couldn't ignore the logic in Nita's words. "So you think I should give Jaime another chance?"

"I think you should at least talk to him face-to-face."

"I'll just be a mess." Liza sniffed. "I've cried so much that my eyes are swollen."

"Good. That will make him even more remorseful, don't you think?"

Liza chuckled. "I'm coming home tomorrow. There's another storm coming through on Tuesday."

"Let's do lunch. I'm headed out to see my family on Tuesday, and I won't be back until New Year's."

"Okay, where do you want to meet?"

"How about I pick something up and come out to your place? I haven't seen your mom in ages."

Liza liked the thought of that. She wasn't ready to go out in public and have one more person ask her details about her engagement and upcoming wedding. "You're a mind reader, Nita. That would be perfect."

"I'll see you tomorrow. Drive safe."

"Thanks, Nita. I'm lucky to have you for a friend."

"I'm luckier."

After Liza hung up, Nita's words kept echoing through her mind. The idea that Jaime had made a huge mistake but that he could still be the right man for her heart was scary to consider. If that was true, what did it mean for their future? Liza had fallen in love with Jaime, and even now, thinking about the time they'd spent together brought the edges of a smile to her face. If she were to forgive him, would they continue dating? Would she be able to truly trust him?

Liza rolled her shoulders back. She didn't have to figure it all out now. She would talk to Nita more about it at lunch tomorrow, and maybe her friend could help her figure out a way to contact Jaime to get the conversation started. Liza nodded, content with her plan. She walked into the kitchen to help Aunt Mary bake her Christmas cake.

Chapter Twenty-Nine

❦

Liza made it back to Echo Ridge by ten o'clock on Monday. It had been hard to leave Mary after their time together, and she promised to visit more often in the future. She had many soul-searching moments and spent a long time on her knees in prayer the previous night. She felt that Nita was right, that it was okay to talk to Jaime and try to sort out everything that had happened. Liza felt safe in considering that route. She kept thinking about Jaime and how she should contact him as she unpacked her suitcase and changed her clothes in preparation for lunch with Nita. Should she text Jaime or call him? Or even drop by his house? Would he even still want to see her, or had he given up completely?

Liza tidied up the kitchen with her mom, and they chatted about the Christmas day menu as they waited for

Nita to arrive. Liza was working on a shopping list when the doorbell rang, and the door opened a half second later, followed by Nita's cheerful hello.

"Nita, it's so good to see you!" Adina said as she hugged her.

"Sorry I've been a stranger. I miss you guys so much. Work just isn't the same without Liza." Nita gave Liza a hug. "How are you feeling today?"

"Better. I think I'm ready to do some hard things."

"Good. I'm glad to hear that, because I really hope you'll forgive me, but someone asked for my help and he seemed pretty desperate, so I told him I'd try my best to help him."

"What?" Liza asked. She heard the front door click open and shut again. A second later, Jaime stood sheepishly in the hallway.

"I told Jaime to come," Nita said. "He just wants to talk to you for a little while, and I really hope you won't be mad at me." Nita licked her lips and scrunched her eyes in an imploring expression. "Your mom was in on it too."

Liza glanced from her mom, to Nita, and then to Jaime. When she saw Jaime, her heart leapt out to him; at the same time, her brain told her to run, or better yet, smack him. She looked at Nita and nodded. "It'll be okay."

"Good, because I'm making lunch with Adina while you and Jaime chat."

Nita kissed Liza's cheek and walked into the kitchen. Adina gave Liza a hug and whispered, "I may have been in on this, but I want you to know that I am here for you. You're my number one priority."

Liza hugged her. "Thanks, Mom."

She turned to face Jaime. He stood in the same place about five paces from the front door. He had his hands in his pockets, and his shoulders were slumped. As she took a step closer, she noticed that his eyes were rimmed with red and he looked weary. She studied him, knowing that the next step she took would be the deciding factor. She could walk toward him, or she could walk away. It wasn't a decision to be made in haste. With a breath, Liza listened to her heart—felt how it reached out toward him. "Jaime."

He lifted his head slightly and took a deep breath. "Liza, I'm so sorry."

"Let's go in the den." Liza led the way into the cozy room by the fireplace. She settled on the large sofa and patted the seat next to her.

"Thank you so much for giving me a chance to talk to you." Jaime sat next to her tentatively. "This has been the worst week of my life."

Liza was about to say the same, but the words died as she thought about what she'd gone through when Mark had called off their engagement. She thought about how she'd suffered as he continued to harass her months after the breakup. Those were lonely, scary times filled with confusion. The situation with Jaime had been horrible, but she was sitting next to him now and didn't feel any of the emotions that she had experienced in relation to Mark. "I was going to agree, but I know you aren't like Mark, and because of that, this wasn't my worst week."

Jaime pressed his lips together, and his eyes filled with moisture. "Liza, I should've trusted you. I didn't know you at first, and I tried to protect Alex—my son—from the chaos and confusion of the divorce and subsequent drama that his mother has put him through. I never agreed to pretend to be your fiancé to benefit myself. I honestly hadn't even considered it until after we were already acting the part. Then I told myself that it probably wouldn't hurt since we were pretending anyway, but by then, I had already started to fall in love with you." He swallowed. "My ex-wife steals my son's medication every chance she gets and he was failing school because of it. I had to get him away from her, so I came up with the idea of boarding school."

Liza covered her mouth with a gasp as she listened to Jaime explain how Kori manipulated and emotionally abused Alex. Tears came to her eyes and Jaime described the home life that his son used to be in. Jaime wiped his eyes. "I'm so very sorry that I lied. I realize now that I could have been truthful with you, but I was afraid to try. And then I wasn't confident enough to just tell you how I felt, because I thought that maybe you would think it was all part of the act." He took her hand and looked in her eyes. "Liza, I love you. Will you please give me a chance to earn your trust?" Jaime took a deep breath and blew it out. "How can I prove to you that what I'm saying is true?"

Liza let Jaime's words fall on her heart like the gentle snowflakes she could see outside the window. She had a choice to make. She could hold out her hand and catch the snowflakes, with a chance to admire the beautiful crystalline structure before they melted, or she could turn away and miss the beauty right in front of her. Liza swallowed and reached out to Jaime, letting his fingers clasp her hand. "Jaime, I fell in love with you, but I've been so confused because I couldn't discern between what was real and what was an act. When I found out that you had lied about your son, I realized that my feelings were true; otherwise, it wouldn't have hurt so much."

Jaime put his arm around her. "I'm so sorry. Can you forgive me?"

Liza nodded. "I already have. I'm more than a little scared, but I can't keep my heart from loving you."

"I love you so much. I'm not sure how I did it, but somehow I prayed you into my life. You're the answer I've been looking for. I would do anything for you, and I was crushed when I thought I'd lost you."

"I don't think you can take all the credit, because I've been praying pretty hard too." Liza smiled. "God certainly has been looking out for me."

Jaime nodded. "No more lies. Only the truth from now on. No acting. Deal?"

"Deal." Liza held out her other hand. Jaime looked at it and pulled her into his arms and kissed her. She wrapped her arms around his neck and returned the kiss, her heart melting like a snowflake in the palm of his hand.

Liza returned Jaime's beautiful ring. They decided that if anyone asked, their response would be that things were still up in the air. They loved each other, but they had kind of done things backwards with the whole engagement.

"I want a chance to do this the right way," Jaime said when he took the ring and put it into his pocket. "I've been thinking a lot over the past few days. And I thought if I had a chance, I wouldn't let it pass without offering you a job."

"A job?" Liza had just given him his ring back, and he was offering her a job?

Jaime chuckled. "I know it's not very romantic, but ulterior motives aside, I want to work with you because I think you're brilliant. You have such a great business sense, and you're not afraid to work hard."

"But how does my skill set work into your business?"

"For one thing, everything that we translate could use a good copy edit, and I do have someone on staff, but we have too much work to do. I've been thinking about bringing in a head editor to train the staff so that we're not only translating accurately but also providing great service to produce the best content possible. There were plenty of other things that I considered as well. Will you think about it?"

Liza grinned. "Yes. I'd love to work with you."

"So is that a yes that you're thinking about it, or ..."

"Yes, and yes."

"That's the second best news I've heard today."

Liza gave him a coy smile. "What was the first best news?"

Jaime pulled her close and kissed her again. "Hearing that you love me."

Chapter Thirty

On Tuesday Jaime had the opportunity to go and visit his son, and he invited Liza to come along, but she opted to wait. There was still a lot of healing that needed to take place between father and son. The custody battle was on hold, but when Kori's attorney had been presented with all the evidence, he softened his stance quite a bit and advised Kori to allow equal shared custody with Alex. Christmas was shaping up to be magical, happy, and full of love.

On Christmas Eve, Liza could barely contain her joy as she waited for Jaime to arrive. He was coming at five o'clock to be there for dinner and their annual Christmas movie marathon. He hadn't seen *It's a Wonderful Life* in over a decade, and Liza insisted that he take part in their family tradition. If they had time, they'd watch *A Christmas Story* and *Elf,* too.

Liza wore a dark green sweater with oversized sleeves accented with a gold necklace and earrings. She had her hair clipped back in loose curls, and she applied her no-smear red lipstick just in case there might be more kissing.

When Jaime arrived, he was carrying an oversized shopping bag. "I brought a little Christmas gift, but you'll have to wait until after dinner."

Liza snapped her fingers. "We're going to have to eat fast, then."

Jaime kissed her cheek and set the bag by the tree. They settled in for a delicious shrimp dinner and ate as Jaime told her parents more about his background and the beauties of Costa Rica.

When everyone was leaning back in their chairs with full stomachs, Jaime looked at Liza with a knowing grin. "Are you ready to open your present?"

"I thought we were supposed to wait until tomorrow to exchange presents," Liza replied innocently.

"Oh no, you don't," Jaime said. "I know you're barely restraining yourself from jumping out of that chair and running over to the Christmas tree right now."

Reuben chuckled. "You know her well."

Liza pretended to pout. "I can wait until Christmas."

Everyone laughed, and Jaime pushed back his chair and helped Liza up from the table. They walked over to the Christmas tree, and Jaime picked up the large shopping bag and pulled out a rather deflated-looking bag of Doritos.

With a giggle, Liza said, "I can see why you made me wait until after dinner now."

"Didn't want to spoil your meal." He handed her the crumpled bag of Nacho Cheese Doritos, complete with a red bow.

With an arched eyebrow, Liza asked, "Did you eat half of this bag already? 'Cause it looks like it's been opened."

Jaime shrugged. "I couldn't help myself."

Liza shook her head and carefully opened the bag. It was not half full of Doritos. In fact, only a few crumbs remained on the inner silver lining of the bag. There was a wrapped gift inside the bag of Doritos. Liza squinted as she pulled out the little box, which had been wrapped in candy-cane-striped paper. "Oh, I wonder if this is from the Candy Counter. It looks suspiciously like their wrapping."

"Go ahead and open it," Jaime said, smiling.

Liza pulled off the wrapping paper and gasped when she recognized the small square shape of a black ring box. She delicately held it, almost afraid to crack open the lid. She lifted her eyes to Jaime's. "What—"

"Just open it, Liza," her mother whispered.

"Oh, okay." For a second, Liza had forgotten that her parents were in the room with them. She ran her hand along the ring box. It had a leather-like finish, and it opened up with a click. Liza gasped. The exquisite sapphire ring surrounded by diamonds was bright and sparkling and beautifully familiar.

Jaime knelt down in front of her. "Liza Marie Sorenson, I love you so much, and I want to spend every happy day with you. Will you marry me?"

Tears filled Liza's eyes and she blinked, trying to focus on the blurry ring and Jaime's handsome face. She covered her mouth with her hand to stifle a sob. Her heart overflowed with joy, because this moment was real. Jaime was in front of her, and he loved her! She felt the truth of his words in her bones, and with a cry she leaned forward and wrapped her arms around his neck.

"Yes," she said. "I love you too. Yes, I'll marry you."

Cheers and sighs from her parents again reminded her that she and Jaime were not alone, but she didn't care. She kissed Jaime with all the feeling she'd held back before, because this kiss was real.

Jaime kissed her and then leaned back, his green eyes filled with emotion. "This is the best Christmas gift I could've imagined."

"Oh, Christmas!" Liza said. She grinned and stepped out of Jaime's embrace. She walked around the side of the Christmas tree and picked up a large gift wrapped in Santa Claus paper. With a barely concealed smile, Liza handed him the big box. "I think you should open this now."

"Are you sure? I don't want to mess up your

Christmas plans just because I decided to propose to you for real this time."

"Just be quiet and open the present." Liza kissed his cheek.

Jaime glanced at Reuben and Adina. "Go ahead," Reuben said.

Adina gave him the thumbs-up sign as she wiped a tear from her cheek.

"Okay, okay." Jaime pulled off the wrapping paper and opened the box. He looked inside and started laughing. Liza joined the laughter, and her parents looked inside the box with confused expressions. There were at least five jumbo bags of Doritos from Costco inside the box.

"What is it with you two and Doritos?" Adina asked.

Jaime pulled Liza close as they laughed. "Good friends always have inside jokes."

Liza kissed him and rested her head on his chest. "I'm so happy that you're finally my fiancé for real."

"I feel the same way," Jaime said, kissing her forehead, "but how long do I have to wait before we can change my title from fiancé to husband?"

Liza tipped her head back. "Hmm, I'm not sure, but that's the last change in title I want you to make." She put her hand on his cheek and looked into his eyes. "Husband. It has a nice ring to it."

Jaime lifted her left hand and touched the ring on her finger. "It certainly does. Merry Christmas, Liza."

Jack's Shack BBQ Chicken Pizza Recipe

Prepare your favorite crust or purchase a pre-made crust. Cauliflower crust is a great option for gluten-free diets.

Ingredients:

1 lb. cooked chicken, chopped or shredded in small pieces

1 bottle of your favorite barbecue sauce, we like honey or Hawaiian BBQ flavor

½ lb bacon cooked and cut into small pieces

1 large can pineapple tidbits, drained

Fresh basil leaves, or use dried if that's all you have

½ lb shredded Mozzarella cheese

½ lb smoked gouda cheese (Optional)

½ red onion, sliced

For perfect pizza crust, first brush the shaped dough lightly with olive oil. This prevents the pizza toppings from making your pizza crust soggy. Using your fingers, push dents into the surface of the dough to prevent bubbling. Top the dough evenly with 1/2 BBQ sauce. Toss the cooked chicken with the remaining BBQ sauce, and then arrange on pizza. Arrange chicken, bacon, red onions, and pineapple over the sauce. Cover with the smoked gouda cheese. Clip basil leaves or place them whole on the pizza.

Bake pizza for 12-15 minutes in a 475 degree oven.

Sneak Peek

H ope for Christmas Sneak Peek
by Rachelle J. Christensen

If you enjoyed this romance from Rachelle J. Christensen, you might like to read the other books in the Echo Ridge Romance series. Enjoy this sneak peek of *Hope for Christmas.*

THE SILVER BELL CHIMED AS ANIKA FLETCHER entered Kenworth's department store. She took two steps forward then stopped when she saw a glint of metal. Crouching, she picked up the quarter next to the toe of her worn black boot. She stamped the last bit of snow from her heels and pocketed the quarter. With only fifty dollars left until the next paycheck, Anika needed every last cent.

"Whatcha got, Mommy?" Four-year-old Megan scrunched her nose and lifted up on her tiptoes.

Anika smiled at her daughter and touched the end of her little pixie nose. "Just a coin."

"We need lots of money so we can pay Beatrice." Megan's voice held no trace of concern.

Anika frowned. Thank goodness her daughter was so even-tempered. The daycare manager, Beatrice, had turned them away fifteen minutes ago.

"I'm sorry dear, I really am. Megan is such a sweetheart but we can't let her stay until you pay your bill. You still owe one-hundred and thirty dollars." Beatrice had given her a look filled with pity before slowly closing the door.

Anika's face heated recalling the humiliating conversation. She felt Megan's tiny fingers wrapping around her hand, and looked down. Megan was like her anchor in the stormy seas. Anika blinked twice, rolled her shoulders back, and smiled at Megan. "It's going to be okay."

She adjusted her name tag and walked past the fragrance counter holding her breath, even inhaling the rich scents seemed too expensive for someone like her. This was a seasonal job, but Anika wanted to work into a full-time position.

They walked past The Candy Counter with its rows and rows of hand-dipped chocolates that made Anika's stomach grumble. She'd skipped lunch, saving the last three slices of bread for Megan. The peanut butter and jelly sandwich she'd made for their dinner called to her from the sack inside her purse.

"Can I have a candy, Mommy?" Megan tugged on Anika's hand.

"Not now. Mommy has to go to work."

Two boys stood next to the display, pointing at the neat row of mint patties. "These are Mom's favorite. Let's get them for Christmas."

The older brother, who looked to be about ten or eleven pointed at the prices. "Tommy, see how much it is a pound? I don't think we have enough." He studied a handful of coins, his lips moving as he counted. "We need seventeen more cents. We could get some of the taffies instead."

"But Mom loves those." Tommy stuck his finger on the glass in front of the mint patties.

Anika hesitated, watching the boys recount their money. She looked over at her daughter and remembered how last week Megan had begged to give a quarter to the Salvation Army bell ringer outside Kenworth's. Anika had clutched tightly to the coin before giving it to Megan. When had she become so hard and tight that she couldn't even let go of a quarter? What hurt more was watching another woman in a beautiful suede coat— likely one of the tourists everyone referred to as *Ice Money*— shush her child and drag him into the store, denying his same request.

She slid the quarter out of her pocket and took a step

closer to the Candy Counter. "Here, this might help you boys. I bet your Mom would love those mint patties."

Tommy looked up and grinned, then glanced at his older brother who studied Anika and the quarter in her outstretched hand. Anika nodded and moved her hand a fraction of an inch closer. The coin wasn't enough to buy a treat for Megan, but maybe it could help the boys. The older boy took the quarter, adding it to his handful of change.

"Thank you." He grinned and both boys turned back to the counter.

Anika smiled, and lifted one shoulder in a half-shrug. She wasn't counting on the quarter anyway, and it was cute to see how excited the boys were. Megan tugged on Anika's other hand and she continued over to the women's department.

Usually Anika parked around back and entered near the offices and employee lounge, but she hadn't figured out what to do about Megan yet. She led her daughter to the checkout station in the women's department, happy that no one had noticed their arrival. Anika stowed the oversized bag full of Megan's toys under the counter and pulled out a few dolls. She cleared a space in the cabinet under the cash register for Megan to play. It was breaking the rules to bring a child to work, but Anika hoped that she could keep Megan quiet and entertained for the next four hours. She was only scheduled to work part-time for the holidays, mostly covering a half-shift. She tried not to think about what she would do next week when she was scheduled for six-hour shifts.

Thankfully Kenworth's wasn't overly busy for a Tuesday, even if it was December first and the Christmas countdown was officially on. The mad rush yesterday on Santa's first day had spiked the store's attendance, but things were slowing down a bit and the man in the red suit had left his throne for a break. Anika shushed Megan each time a customer approached and did her best to keep up with her duties in the women's department.

Megan munched on her peanut butter sandwich, looked at books, and played with her toys, but by eight o'clock she was tired and Anika had run out of ideas.

"I want gummies!" Megan stamped her foot and cried.

"Shh, Meg. We have to be very quiet so we don't scare the shoppers," Anika infused a soothing tone into her voice, but it wasn't very convincing. Her own stomach tightened, grumbling with the gnawing hunger that she'd grown accustomed to. A pack of gummies, or any food right at the moment would be welcome. Anika picked Megan up and rocked her back and forth, humming along to the tune of *Silent Night* playing over the sound system.

Anika saw her boss round the corner and wished she could climb under one of the racks of designer clothes she'd just arranged. The woman had steel gray hair, a temper that matched it, and eyebrows that were perpetually arched in a slant of disgust with everyone and everything she came in contact with.

Cecilia Grange, acting CEO of Kenworth's Department store walked toward Anika and pointed her long finger at Megan. "I take it this is your daughter?"

"Yes, I apologize," Anika's voice was just above a whisper. "I didn't have another option tonight."

"Was she the one I just heard crying? We don't want to annoy our patrons." Cecilia's strident tone made it clear who was annoyed.

"I'm really sorry. I've got her settled down now." Anika turned so that Cecilia could see Megan's angelic face. Her daughter smiled at Cecilia just as Anika had hoped. She saw her boss soften a fraction.

Cecilia's eyebrow lowered a millimeter. "Well, as long as she's quiet, I guess we can make an exception."

Anika didn't promise that it would never happen again because she still hadn't figured out what to do with Megan tomorrow during her shift. "Thank you. She's really a good little girl and won't cause any trouble."

Cecilia pursed her lips. "I came to talk to you about the overtime you signed up for. Are you still capable of filling it?"

"Yes, I'd be glad to help however I can." Anika tried to tone down the desperate eagerness she heard in her voice.

"We're setting up a giving tree," Cecilia said. "It's one of Keira's projects." She rolled her eyes and huffed as though Keira's ideas were only meant to torture her. "I'm going along with it because I have to humor some people. After the store closes tonight I need you to set up the tree."

Anika swallowed hard and nodded. "I can certainly do that."

"Then you'll need to decorate it and help with the handmade cards we're creating to hang on the tree. We have an association that will be supplying names of those in need this holiday season." Cecilia pointed at a long box on the other side of the counter. "The tree is in there. We want it completed by tomorrow night."

"I can do that." Anika shifted Megan in her arms. Thankfully, her daughter remained quiet, probably scared silent by Cecilia's eyebrows.

Cecilia glanced at Megan and back at Anika. "Good."

After the tapping of her heels faded, Anika looked at the box holding the Christmas tree and groaned. Anika's stomach grumbled, protesting the lack of food. It was going to be a long night.

"Megan, honey, move your dolls and car back behind the counter." Anika pointed at the toys she'd nearly tripped over on her way to unbox the Christmas tree.

"Okay, Mommy, in a minute," Megan answered, and then continued talking to her dolls.

It was nine o'clock and Kenworth's was officially closed. Anika was tired but she still had to straighten the changing rooms and count out her till. Megan should've been in bed an hour ago, but since her little tantrum she'd been good-natured about playing in the cupboards and shelves behind the counter.

Anika stooped and ripped the packing tape off the box. The artificial tree burst from its confines like a Jack-in-the-box, startling her. She sucked in a breath and put a hand over her heart. There were dozens of branches with color-tipped ends. She couldn't see the trunk though it must be in there somewhere. The tree was squished and flat. It would take a degree in engineering to figure this thing out.

"Stupid Christmas tree," she muttered. If it weren't for Megan, she'd skip Christmas altogether. The holiday was a slap in the face to someone like Anika— a divorced, single mom with a deadbeat ex. She hadn't been able to locate Jimmy after he'd been released from jail the last time, but she was tired of hiding from him. When she moved to Echo Ridge a year ago, she decided a fresh start would be the best solution to her problems. The sleepy little New York town had been full of promises and hope, but after losing her job two months ago when Megan was hospitalized with pneumonia, everything had changed. Although the state had helped pay for Megan's treatment, Anika had fallen farther and farther behind.

Her chest tightened when she thought about what was around the next corner. This job was temporary, and Anika had run out of options. If she didn't find something soon, she'd be evicted from her one bedroom apartment.

She pulled the tree trunk upright and began putting together the sections of the tree. It took much longer than it should have with bits of the white flock crumbling and sticking to her clothes. One of the branches refused to straighten, the end was all twisted and it took her nearly ten minutes to smooth out the kinks. Anika grumbled to herself about the fake tree and its apparent mission to annoy her by not snapping together correctly. She fiddled with the pre-lit strands that had to be connected in several places. There were three different cords to test the lights, but she couldn't get them all to work together. The box said the lights were supposed to twinkle, but Anika couldn't even get more than one strand to turn on at a time. She grumbled and stepped back— on Megan's dolls. Anika's foot turned, she gasped, and fell forward into the tree with a shriek.

Before she could react to the fake evergreen needles poking her in the face, strong hands pulled her back from the mass of lights and cords.

"Are you hurt?"

Anika blinked and looked up at the man who had spoken. Her mouth opened and closed, and she shook her head. If Enrique Iglesias had come to her rescue then she was definitely going to thank the blasted Christmas tree. She rubbed a hand over her face and saw that he wasn't Enrique, but with the shadow of scruff along his chin and his slightly mussed black hair against caramel skin, he could be Enrique's younger brother. Anika shook her head. She was gawking, and hadn't answered his question. "I'm not sure," she said.

"Let's get you away from this tree. I don't think it likes you." He cupped his hand under her forearm, carefully lifting her off the ground.

Anika winced when she put weight on her foot. "Ouch. I kind of twisted my ankle."

"Sit down right here and I can take a look at it." His dark hair matched his chocolate brown eyes and Anika found herself wondering again if Enrique did have a younger brother.

He helped her sit, leaning next to the wood paneling of her checkout station. He crouched down and held out his hand. "I'm Carlos Rodriguez. I'm a volunteer fireman, so I have some medical training. Mind if I take a look?" He had a Spanish accent, not heavy, but alluring, and Anika listened to him appreciatively.

"Oh, it's just my ankle. I'm sure it'll be fine in a few minutes." Anika winced again when she moved her toes. "My name's Anika Fletcher." She held out her hand and Carlos shook it, his grip firm, yet gentle at the same time. Anika tore her eyes away from him and reached down to examine her ankle. It didn't appear to be swelling, but every tendon around the bone ached. Maybe she should have him look at it. "Ugh, this is just what I didn't need tonight." She leaned over and massaged the tender side of her ankle. It wouldn't cost her anything to have him look at it. "Okay, maybe I'd better have you look." She moved back so that Carlos could see her ankle.

He leaned over and gently pulled her pant leg up. His fingers were warm, and he pressed lightly around her ankle. Anika's heart sped up— it was hard to ignore the flutter in her stomach as he carefully examined her foot. He looked over at her and smiled. "There might be a little swelling later, but it's a good sign that it's not turning colors. You need to ice it and wrap it to stabilize the area."

Anika let out the breath she'd been holding when he released her foot. "Okay, thanks for your help. I was trying to get that dang tree figured out. It definitely doesn't like me and the feeling is mutual."

Carlos walked over to the tree, now standing almost ten feet tall, and shifted a few branches. Then he crouched down by the electrical outlet. "You know, this could be considered a fire hazard."

Anika straightened and leaned forward to look at the surge protector. Had she plugged in too many cords? She scrunched her nose counting the four cords snaking from the tree to the power source. "I didn't think that was too many." She looked over at him.

Carlos grinned. He was teasing her! And his smile

made those dark eyes light up— the ones that were looking at her with appreciation.

Anika smiled, started to lean forward, but then she pulled back abruptly. "Thanks for your help. I'd better get back to work." She gave her head a little shake, reminding herself that *all* men were off limits no matter how closely they were related to Enrique Iglesias.

"The store's closed. Aren't you about finished?" Carlos glanced around the empty department store.

Anika followed his gaze to the flickering light above the toys and strollers in the back of the store. Beyond that light in the back offices, Cecilia was probably still hard at work, and Anika couldn't afford to be caught sitting around. "Yes, I'm just putting in some overtime to get this tree set up."

Carlos crouched next to the tree and fiddled with the cords. "This must be new. I don't remember seeing a tree set up in this department last year." When Anika gave him a curious look, he explained. "I've done a lot of the remodeling in this store over the past few years." Carlos thumbed behind him. "I'm finishing up some shelves over in the children's section this week."

"Oh, I noticed those. They look really nice," Anika said. She forced herself to turn her gaze from Carlos's muscular shoulders to the remodeling of the children's section. There were three rows of new shelves against the wall, the light oak wood spanning a length of about five feet. She could imagine how nice it would be to display different items.

"Thanks," Carlos's voice was muffled. "Now, let's see if that works."

He flipped the switch and the tree lit up with twinkling white lights.

"You fixed it," Anika said. She hopped closer to the tree and touched one of the white lights. "Thank you."

Carlos chuckled. "Glad I could help." He straightened the tree and turned to Anika. "How's your ankle?"

"It's a little tender, but I think it will be fine." Anika held herself carefully so as not to put too much weight on her foot. Her curiosity motor was spinning rapidly over the fireman who'd just saved her and the Christmas tree. The way he stood there with that bit of coarse stubble lining his jaw made her want to reach out and touch it. No, wait. She clenched her hands into fists. She most certainly did not want to touch him, or any man for that matter.

This was Kenworth's and she was an employee, she needed to focus. She wiped her hand over her mouth, straightened her shoulders and said, "Thanks again for your help. I'd better finish up now."

"How much work do you have left tonight? I'll probably be here for another hour." Carlos smiled at her and she could almost see the wheels in his mind turning. He looked like he was on the verge of asking her out. She didn't have time for this.

"Well, I'm hoping to be finished soon because my daughter—" Anika stopped talking and turned toward the cash register. "Megan!" She hadn't heard a sound from her daughter for the past several minutes while she was caught up ogling forbidden territory.

Anika scrambled around the counter. Megan wasn't there. She looked up and met Carlos's gaze, his eyes searched hers, and she could see her panic mirrored there for an instant.

"Your daughter?" he came around the corner and scanned the floor littered with Megan's toys.

"She was right here playing. She's four, with brown hair and blue eyes— looks just like me. I'll check the break room." Anika moved to pass Carlos, but he stopped her, putting a hand on her arm.

"Wait, what's that?" he pointed to the corner of a pink and white polka-dotted blanket hanging out of the cupboard under the register—Megan's blanket.

Anika's breath caught in her throat and her heart double-timed, pounding against her rib cage. She crouched and opened the cupboard. The breath whooshed out of her when she saw Megan curled up with her blanket, sleeping in the cramped space among rolls of receipt paper, sacks, and cloth shopping bags. Anika sat back on the floor and squeezed her eyes shut. "Thank goodness."

She felt a hand on her back and looked over to see

Carlos crouching next to her. "She's cute. That's quite a hiding place."

"My word, that scared me to death. I'm so glad you saw her blanket. Thank you." Anika moved to stand, but her ankle didn't cooperate and she stumbled into Carlos.

His arms moved around her, quickly righting her and then letting her go. "Do you need help getting her to your car? I don't mind carrying her."

Anika opened her mouth to say no, but with her ankle she'd have to accept his help. Her mind was still a few seconds behind, feeling the strength of his arms as he caught her, the solid muscles of his body holding her upright. *Focus, Anika!* She glanced at the clock. It was already past ten, she was exhausted. "I guess I'll finish the tree tomorrow night. Are you sure you don't mind carrying her?"

Carlos grinned. "Not at all. A fireman is trained to complete his rescues."

"Well, you've saved me twice tonight," Anika replied. She was gushing, and thanking this guy way too much. He was just being polite. She needed to get a grip and quit smiling at him. But every time she smiled, he would smile back and it made her stomach do a little flip that she was sure meant trouble.

"It's my pleasure. Do you think she'll wake up when I lift her?" he crouched next to Megan's sleeping form.

"I would be very surprised. She sleeps like a rock. Her

name's Megan." Anika said. "Let me just grab my things here."

"You might want to turn off the tree for the night. Cecilia warned me not to overload the circuits. I guess the electrical wiring in this building is pretty old."

Anika nodded and flipped off the lights. She watched as Carlos gently knelt next to her daughter and lifted Megan into his arms. The child sighed and pulled her blanket tighter. Carlos held her tenderly and smiled, lifting his eyes to meet Anika's. The way he held her so carefully did something dangerous to Anika's heart. It was like the moment a match slides across the side of the box igniting an explosion of heat that pops and sizzles. And she couldn't afford to play with fire.

Keep reading *Hope for Christmas*, available in ebook, print, and audio. For more information visit

www.rachellechristensen.com

Acknowledgments

"I keep making plans for my life, but there's always some plot twist I didn't expect, so I'm trying to roll with it." I fully agree with Liza! I wrote this book three months after breaking my back in a diving accident that required major surgery and fusion of five vertebrae. I stood the entire time I wrote this novel because my loving husband found me a standing desk platform and then helped me brainstorm the story. I wasn't sure that I would be able to write this book, but through lots of prayer and tons of help from my family, I reached my goal.

I want to thank my wonderful writing friends. I have been blessed to be part of a wonderful writing community for over a decade and the friendship and support they give me is amazing. I especially want to thank Janet Halling for offering to beta read my next novel when I was in a place where no words would come. Her support and encouragement helped me during some very low times.

Big thanks to my beta readers and editors, Janet Halling, Cathy Jeppsen, Jenna Roundy, Tyler H., and Tim Jolley.

Family is the ultimate gift and I feel so blessed to have mine! My children are an incredible source of inspiration, noise, laughter, and love. I love you and how you cheer me on when I'm writing. Thanks to my husband, Tyler, for encouraging me to write and believing in me—it was so fun to outline this story together.

I am grateful for my loving Heavenly Father who has helped me grow so much in this past year while carrying me through my trials. All goodness comes from God, and I'm thankful for the knowledge I have that helps me make sense of my own life story.

I wrote this book for many reasons and the most important is you, dear reader, because I am just like you—a reader at heart. Thank you for choosing to read my book and for your continued support of my creative works. I hope that we can enjoy many more stories together in the future!

About the Author

Photo by Erin Summerill

Rachelle writes mystery/suspense, clean romance, and women's fiction. She is the mother of a large family and she solves the case of the missing shoe on a daily basis. She enjoys raising chickens, laughing with her family, and traveling with her husband. She graduated cum laude from Utah State University with a degree in psychology and a minor in music.

Rachelle is the award-winning author of over twenty books, including *The Soldier's Bride (a Kindle Scout Selection)*, the Rone award winner for mystery, *River Whispers*, *Diamond Rings Are Deadly Things*, *Hawaiian Masquerade*, and *the Echo Ridge Romance series*. Her novella, "Silver Cascade Secrets," was included in the Rone Award–winning *Timeless Romance Anthology, Fall Collection*.

Join Rachelle's VIP mailing list to learn more about upcoming books and get your free book at www.rachellechristensen.com.

Free Book!